Bootful of Echoes

Kay Springsteen

δ

Dingbat Publishing

BOOTFUL OF ECHOES
Copyright © 2014 Kay Springsteen
ISBN 978-1-940520-31-5

Published by Dingbat Publishing
Humble, Texas

Back cover photo © 123rf.com and peterdenovo
Front cover photo © 123rf.com and Olivier Le Queinec

Other Books by Kay Springsteen

The Echoes of Orson's Folly
Lifeline Echoes
Elusive Echoes
Abiding Echoes

The Heart Stories
Heartsight
Camp Wedding
Heartsent
Heartfelt
Operation: Christmas Hearts
The 13 of Hearts

Regencies
The Toymaker
Teach Me Under the Mistletoe

With Kim Bowman
A Lot Like a Lady
Something Like a Lady
"Inner Flame" in anthology Kick Ass Chicks

Dedication

With love and gratitude to my Lord and Savior, Jesus Christ, from whom I draw my life, my love, and my inspiration. Happy Birthday!

With fond memories of Christmases past and Christmases yet to come, this book is dedicated to my readers everywhere, for your support and your encouragement. And with love to my sisterheart, Cindi Q., for the love we share and because you've always been there for me. May the beauty that is your spirit always live on this earth in Perfect Harmony.

Chapter One

The sugary aroma of something baking greeted Justin at the back door. It didn't even matter what it was — his sweet tooth demanded a taste, and his mouth watered in anticipation. As he stepped through and closed the door against the blast of December air, he inhaled deeply and smiled. His daughter-in-law hummed to herself as she pulled a tray of individual pies from the oven and set them on top of the range to cool.

The smile tugged Justin's lips farther upward. Except for hair the color of dark chocolate rather than sunny blond, she reminded him of his Beth — right down to the frilly apron worn over her blue jeans and Western shirt, and hair put up in a messy ponytail. Even her red-tipped bare toes peeking out from the hem of her jeans reminded him of his late wife. Ryan had won a good one when Sandy had said yes.

Justin removed his hat and parked it on one of the hooks next to the door, then shrugged out of his coat. "Sandy, my sweet girl, please tell me that's dessert for tonight and not more goodies for the church."

The humming stopped and she glanced over her shoulder. "I'll make a deal with you," she countered, using the back of one hand to swipe at a strand of hair falling across her eyes.

Wariness crept over him as he sized her up. "Deal?" he asked, hoping he wasn't showing too much interest with the question. He'd never been able to shake the feeling that her deals somehow bested him every time.

"Brother Bobby called earlier. They needed a couple more desserts for the homebound Christmas dinners. Since Ryan and Sean took the SUV to Cheyenne, Ricky's going to use Ryan's truck to get these pies into Orson's Folly." She caught him up in her sunny smile. "If you go with, you can help him, and then the two of you can pick up a few things at the market for Christmas Eve dinner on Wednesday, and I'll have time to make a couple of pies for dessert tonight."

Justin's stomach rumbled in protest that he'd have to drive all the way to town smelling those pies without so much as a slice. But he nodded. At least he'd have something to look forward to when he got home. "Okay, give me time to get some of the barn smell off me. Where is Ricky, anyway? I saw Ryan's truck out there."

"Changing out of his school clothes." She picked up a flattened white box and began to unfold it. "I'll have these pies boxed up by the time you're both ready."

After a last longing glance at the six freshly baked pies lined up on the counter, Justin heaved a sigh and headed for the stairs. Ricky met him at the top step.

"Hey, Dad."

"I'm tagging along on your run into town," said Justin, with his hand on his doorknob.

"Yeah, Sandy told me."

A chuckle slipped out. "She did, huh?" So the "deal" had been planned all along. He might have known. "Good of her to let me know."

Ricky shot him a giant grin. "I didn't know I was recruited until ten minutes ago."

Twenty minutes later they were on the road. On their way out, Sandy had handed Ricky the boxes of pies and Justin a bag of oatmeal chocolate chip cookies, with stern instructions to share. He bit into one as he relaxed back into the passenger seat of his oldest son's four-door pickup. "Umm.

Still warm." After they hit the main road, he held out the bag for Ricky.

"Thanks." The cookie disappeared in two bites.

"How's school? You out for the holidays now?"

"Almost."

Oh, hell, was it going to be one of *those* rides? The kind where Justin did all the talking and Ricky answered in grunts and single words? It couldn't still be uneasiness about his adoption. He'd had most of the year to get used to that.

"You gonna make me play guessing games all the way to town, or do you plan to tell me what's eating you at some point?" Justin snagged another cookie and sat back in the seat as he munched. And waited.

Bob Seger rocked *The Little Drummer Boy* on the radio for a couple of miles before Elvis crooned about his Christmas being blue.

Seven miles passed, by Justin's estimation. The music segued into Mariah Carey claiming she only wanted one thing for Christmas. They only had another twenty miles or so before they hit the outskirts of Orson's Folly. Justin could wait the boy out. He'd had plenty of practice, waiting on his older sons over the years. As John Lennon finished singing about war being over, a male voice took up the story of a little boy trying to buy his mother a pair of shoes.

"Crickets on crackers," muttered Justin, and he stabbed the OFF button on the radio before he found himself blubbering. "When did Christmas get so dang depressing?"

A heavy sigh answered him.

Ahh, should have turned the radio off two songs ago. The gusty sigh sounded like he might be in line for a weighty conversation. That called for another cookie, so Justin grabbed one from the bag.

"Natalie isn't coming out after Christmas."

It was Justin's turn to sigh, but he suppressed it. The girl's absence might not be such a bad thing, since his youngest son had a crush on her and she was still a tender age.

"I mean, Mel's gonna miss her, ya know?"

Yeah. Mel might miss her biological daughter, but after all, she and Sean were chasing after a healthy seventeen-month-old son these days, so they weren't alone. Besides, according to Sean, Mel and the girl she'd given birth to as a teenager chatted on the computer just about every other night.

"You know, Natalie has her own family," Justin pointed out quietly then nibbled on the edge of his cookie.

Another half mile passed without a comment.

He tried again. "Might be the Carters have their own family traditions on holidays."

That elicited a grunt.

Fact was, Ricky was probably more disappointed for himself and the plans he and Natalie had made for her next visit. Of course, telling him that would do no good. Not only was Ricky a teenager, he was a bullheaded one. What the boy needed was a distraction.

"Pull in at AJ's, will you?"

The mute double take was almost Saturday morning cartoon-worthy. "What about the pies?"

Justin spared a glance over his shoulder at the picnic cooler secured on the vinyl seat with the seatbelt. An infant couldn't be much safer than those fruity delights. "Well, unless Sandy baked legs on them, I have doubts they'll up and walk away."

Ricky steered the truck into the postage stamp-sized parking lot and edged into one of the many open spaces. "What're you gettin' here?" he asked, leaning over the steering wheel and squinting at the front of the store through the windshield.

"Just a few last-minute things." Justin popped the door open and slid to the ground, wincing at the jarring sensation that vibrated up his legs to the rest of his body. Getting old sucked. He pushed the door closed and headed for the long wooden porch. A burst of icy wind blew a few flurries along the gravel underfoot.

Ricky stepped out of the truck but didn't immediately shut the door. "I thought you were all done shopping."

Justin tossed a glance over his shoulder. "Depends what you mean by shopping, I guess. You coming or not?"

Giving a half-assed shrug, the boy slammed the pickup door. His long strides closed the gap between them, and they hit the deserted porch at about the same time.

"You see the display at City Hall this year?" Justin tugged the door open.

A snicker accompanied Ricky over the threshold.

Oh, yeah, he'd seen it. Of course, since he worked in town at the local bar, it would be hard for him to miss it.

"It's so lame," mumbled the boy. "I think it gets worse every year."

Pausing at the candy carousel, Justin faced his son. "Can you keep a secret?"

Interest sparked in Ricky's eyes. "What kind of secret?"

That deserved a mental kick to the head. The boy'd grown up keeping all kinds of secrets — nasty ones, the kind that ate into the soul.

"I think that sorry light show ought to have itself a sprucing." He angled his head. "Thing is, I'm not inclined to make a big production out of it."

Ricky screwed up his face. "What does that even mean?"

A sigh slipped past Justin's lips as he fought against rolling his eyes. "What do you think it means?" He grabbed a shopping cart and headed for the holiday decorations along the store's front wall. "It means we're going on a secret mission."

A glance over his shoulder showed Ricky standing stock still, staring as though he thought Justin had lost his mind. Justin waggled his eyebrows. "What do you say, boy? You in or out?"

One hesitant step forward, followed by another, a bit more sure. "What do I have to do?" And Ricky was in.

Justin shrugged. "By the time we drop off the pies, City Hall ought to be closed up. We'll just pick up a few things and add a little pizzaz to the display... liven up the show."

He studied the shelves. For being so close to the holiday, AJ's still had a good selection of decorations in stock. Justin slipped a white box with red lettering off the top of a tall stack and looked at the multi-colored bulbs with a grunt.

"What do you think? Colors? Or classic white?"

A grin worked its way over Ricky's face. "Both?"

"I like the way you think." Justin dropped the box into the cart and grabbed the rest of the stack. Ignoring Ricky's gaping mouth, he sidestepped to the next row and grabbed the stack of all-white lights. "Extension cords..." he mumbled, scanning the shelves.

"Hey, what about... ah..." Ricky gestured to an oversized nativity scene marked fifty percent off.

"You know, used to be a town could set up a religious scene on public property." Justin shook his head. "These days, people take offense at that. Seems like if they can celebrate the day, they ought to celebrate what makes it a holiday."

"I was—" Ricky cleared his throat and drew a deep breath. "The church doesn't have anything but a string of lights around the sign..."

Justin's breath stalled, and a smile slid over his face. The kid was becoming invested. "You want to light up Brother Bobby's church?"

"Kinda..." One shoulder lifted then fell. "Yeah, I do."

Why not? Justin nodded at the set. "Grab it. Hitting the church ought to be easy. We're already going there with the pies."

Two overloaded shopping carts later, they were ready to check out. Justin tried not to think about how much lighter his bank account would be when they left. After all, it was for a worthy cause.

"Um... what about AJ?" asked Ricky, peering around the end of the aisle. "He's gonna know who bought all this stuff."

"You let me worry about AJ," said Justin, digging out his wallet. "Anyone else up there?"

Ricky peeked again and shook his head. "Mr. Tenbaum just left— Oh, shit! I mean crap. I mean... Ms. Charlie's crossing the parking lot."

"Well, dang." That would put a crimp in the plan. Charlotte Hains had been his best friend since childhood. And she was a lot of things, but dumb wasn't one of them. The sharp-eyed cook had undoubtedly recognized the truck, so she'd be looking for a McGee in the store. If she found him cornering the market on AJ's Christmas decorations, his secret would be out. "Why isn't she working?" He slipped a twenty from his wallet and held it out it to his son. "Catch her at the door and get her to help you find a Christmas present for someone."

The stunned expression that settled over Ricky's face as he stared at the money would have been comical on any other occasion. They didn't have time for comical. Charlie would be on a mission once she hit the door. He stuffed the bill into Ricky's hand and gave him a little shove.

Casting a slightly irritated glance over his shoulder, Ricky stepped into the main aisle. "Hey, Ms. Charlie!"

"Ricky, what are you doing here? Are you with Sandy?"

"Ah... um, no. I'm, ah, shopping. For Christmas... Could you help me with a present?"

"Shopping? For whom?"

Their voices grew distant and Justin risked a peek around the aisle cap, catching sight of the pair heading toward the rear of the store. Ricky reached behind his back and sent a thumbs-up signal.

That was the cue to haul the carts to the register.

"Looks like you cleaned me out." A huge grin lifted AJ's mouth. "Spreading a little Christmas cheer again, McGee?"

"I don't know what you're talking about. Thought we'd decorate the Cross MC a little bit." Justin laid his debit card on the counter as AJ scanned the purchases. He was ahead of Justin by a few years, with charcoal gray and silver hair that mostly only covered the sides of his head. His handlebar mustache was something right out of the Gay Nineties, though it was a recent affectation that had come about after he'd expanded part of his store into an old time candy shop and ice cream parlor. Justin couldn't recall a year when his friend wasn't trying some new marketing gimmick.

AJ twirled one end of his mustache and wiggled an eyebrow suggestively. "And I'm sure the, uh... *cows* will appreciate your efforts." He quickly bagged up the lights then ran the card and handed it back. "Leo's got some nice greens over at the Feed and Tack. Those cedar ropes that look real nice looped over... stockyard fences. I'll give him a call and get you set up with some." He loaded the purchases into the cart and headed for the door. "I gave you half off everything."

"Thanks!" Justin shot AJ a grin and peered toward the back of the store. "Ah... my boy's entertaining Charlie. Try to keep her occupied until he gets out to the truck?"

"You got it."

Chapter Two

Three votes of no, one nose wrinkle, and a grunt later, and Charlie's blood pressure was probably soaring out of control, if the heat edging the tips of her ears was any indication. It didn't help that the store's sound system was blaring that stupid hippopotamus song that tended to get stuck in her brain.

Ricky shook his head — that made "no" number four — and put down the pink sweater he'd been holding for several minutes. "No... I don't think so. I mean, what does a sweater say?"

"What does it say?" she repeated, giving in to her confusion. "Hopefully nothing. My clothes start talking to me, I'm gonna need meds in high dosages."

The boy rolled his eyes. "I mean, what kind of statement does a sweater make as a gift?"

"Well, since you won't tell me who it's for, I don't know." She huffed out a breath. So much for her quick errand. Her break was going to be used up and then some by the time she got through with *helping* Ricky. "What kind of statement do you *want* it to make?"

His face took on a pained look as he shrugged. "I dunno... just... something."

It was time — past time — to help him along. "Okay, is this for a special gal? Someone you've been seeing?"

"Yeah... well, not really. Just... you know. Someone I know." He scuffed one boot back and forth over the worn plank flooring.

"Well, does she have any particular interests? Does she like to do anything special? Does she have a favorite color?" *Some people just shouldn't ever shop for gifts.* She picked up a blue and white hat, scarf, and mitten set. "This is pretty. Nice and soft, but very practical. I just stopped by to get a few for the Jesse tree at church."

Ricky's face twisted as he angled his head and studied the set. Well, at least that was a new expression.

A familiar soft chuckle reached her ears. Was that Justin? It sounded like it was coming from the front of the store. She moved toward the end of the aisle to see if she could spot him.

"Hey! Ms. Charlie, do hats come in sizes?" called Ricky.

"Huh?" Her steps faltered. "Oh, um, no. One size usually fits all."

"Really?" He picked up a gray set and stared at the hat. "Can you, like, try this on for me so I can see?"

She sighed and walked back to where Ricky waited. So much for visiting with Justin. If that even *had* been Justin.

"Is your dad with you?" she asked, forcing a casual tone, though she hadn't been feeling particularly casual around Justin lately.

"Is my dad with me?" It was apparently Ricky's turn to be repetitive. "Uh..." He glanced around. "Is he here?"

Charlie expelled another exasperated breath. "Never mind. I thought I heard him, but if he's not with you, it must have been someone else."

A bell jingled from the front of the store — someone coming or going. As requested, Charlie stretched the hat over her head. Great, she'd go back to work with hat hair. She looked up. "Well, what do you...?"

Ricky was at the aisle's end and moving.

"Ricky?" She raised her voice. "What about the hat?"

"It looks nice," he called back. "Well, I gotta go now."

"But—" Scowling, she yanked the hat off. "—what about the present you need help with?"

He shot her a nervous glance. "Oh, um... I just remembered. I already got her something. Gotta go. Bye!" He disappeared around the corner.

She stared at the empty aisle. "Wha-a-at the *hell*... was that?"

As she dropped the hat set into her cart to give to the church, Charlie paused. AJ had quite a few in stock, and they *were* nice and soft. She scooped an assortment from the display and dropped them into the shopping basket that held her purse. Hopefully she'd find their counterparts in the men's department.

The aisle's end cap had a display of similar sets in children's sizes. A smile worked its way onto Charlie's face as she set an assortment of those in her cart as well. Then it was time to check out.

"Afternoon, Ms. Charlie." AJ smiled from behind the register. "Looks like you're outfittin' half the population of Orson's Folly."

"Oh..." An uneasy giggle escaped. "More like a third. I was getting some for the Jesse tree at church when it hit me that maybe I should drop a few off at the schools."

"Well, now, that's a fine idea. I know my Susie says half the time her students come to school not dressed for the weather." He shook his head. "You'd think folks living in these parts would have the sense to dress their children for the cold... but then Susie said lots of 'em can't afford it. I reckon your gift'll be truly appreciated."

A sigh of relief snuck out. He'd just confirmed her idea was a sound one. "That's good to know. But, ah... let's just keep this between us, okay?"

AJ painstakingly scanned each item and placed them in bags. When the total popped up on the register, Charlie blinked. "That can't be correct. It's far too low."

"Holiday discount," said AJ, twirling one end of his fancy mustache.

The air seemed to leave her in a rush. "Why... thank you. I appreciate that very much."

He winked, and a smile sprang to Charlie's lips. If not for Susie, AJ's beloved wife, Charlie might have taken his flirting seriously. But it had been love at first sight between the storekeeper and the young fourth grade schoolteacher who'd shown up in Orson's Folly one summer more than three decades back. And they'd set about expanding the population yearly for a dozen years to prove it.

At least their holidays won't be lonely... The wistful thought drifted in like feathers on the wind. Surely at least a couple of their children would show up, their own burgeoning families in tow. She sighed. Unlike her own girls, all seeming to be scattered to the winds and all having other plans for this holiday season.

"Got that order in yesterday and delivered it for you." AJ's casual words as he set the last bag of winter sets into her shopping cart brought Charlie out of her sad thoughts.

"And it all went as planned?"

"Couldn't have been smoother."

"Thanks, AJ." She looped the bags over her arms and headed for the door. A gust of wind shoved it back in her face. "Dang, something nasty's brewin' out here."

"I heard tell there's a storm blowing through, but it's mostly gonna hold to the north," said AJ as he rushed to assist with the door. He peered at the sky and shook his head. "Don't look like it's got much for us, but I'm glad tomorrow's the last day of school until after the holidays."

That meant she ought to drop off her little gifts before she went back to finish her shift at Valentine's. They could be handed out the next day. Well, Luke was pretty easygoing and Mondays weren't so busy that the new guy, Steve, couldn't handle rustling up an order or two. Especially since Bertie was there to help.

She loaded the last bag onto the back seat of her car and stepped into another burst of biting cold wind. She peered at the whitish sky. AJ was right, though; it didn't look heavy with snow, so the storm would probably miss them. Even if it didn't, though, it wasn't any concern to her. She had nowhere to go for Christmas, so it would be no trouble at all, holing up in her little house in town. Her pantry had been stocked for the past week, long before the Christmas rush. And she'd had two cords of firewood delivered that morning. A visit to the library the day before had expanded her reading pile. All nice and cozy. The only thing she was missing was a nice cat to curl up with in front of the fire.

She pulled up at the elementary school and set the brake on her SUV. Half walking, half sliding along the walkway up to the door, she pictured a nice tabby cat. Why shouldn't she have companionship? Her hours at Valentine's had been cut back at her request. Just seemed like there should be more to life than working and feeding paying customers.

The Cross MC always seemed to have kittens about. Maybe she could take one of them in. They were barn cats, sure, but if she got one young enough, maybe it would adjust. Couldn't hurt to try. Once she made that decision, her steps seemed lighter. She rang the buzzer for admission into the building and stared into the camera so the secretary could see her face. When the door lock released with a loud clank, she grabbed the handle and pulled.

Once inside, she was immediately confronted with a red-lettered sign ordering all visitors to report directly to the principal's office. A thick black arrow pointed to the left. The soft scuffling sounds of her boots on the linoleum broke through the hush as she headed in that direction. The school was as oddly familiar as it was strangely foreign. She'd grown up wandering these halls, spent more time in the office than she should have. Then as a mom she'd attended all over again in the form of room mother helper. And now, here she was yet again, only this time with no friends or family attending school there. Kind of made her feel like an interloper.

The rustle of the bags she carried reminded her of her mission. Pasting a smile on her face, she pushed open the office door and stepped back in time. She almost expected to see her usual partner in crime, Justin McGee, sitting in one of the chairs lining the wall to the right of the door.

School secretary Betty Bowman raised her head and slid her computer keyboard tray beneath the desk. With a smile of greeting, she patted her steel-gray hair and stood. "Merry Christmas, Charlie. What can I do for you today?"

"I ran into a sale on some winter gear at AJ's and I thought I'd drop a few bags off here. Maybe you can hand them out as gifts?"

Betty's eyes lit up. "Oh, how wonderful! We're having a school-wide holiday festival tomorrow. That'll be the perfect time. And someone else dropped off a load of new book bags just the other day."

Charlie blinked. "Really? Who?"

"Why, I have no idea," murmured Betty, clearing space for Charlie's packages on a long conference table. "They were left out on the loading dock with a note." She sighed. "Isn't it lovely? People doing for others like this?"

"Yes... well, can I count on you to keep my little gift a secret?"

"Oh, sure!" Betty giggled like a little girl. "Mum's the word."

Charlie didn't linger, though she suspected Betty would have shot the breeze until school let out. Her car keys jingled as she hiked back to her car, feeling pretty pleased with herself. Betty had truly seemed to have no clue where the new backpacks had come from. Her secret arrangement with AJ remained a secret — even from the school staff.

The combination middle school and high school was only a couple of blocks over from the elementary school, so Charlie made short work of dropping off her gifts. This time, no one needed to tell her about backpacks. Two large crates from the box store in Jackson stood outside the office, open and showing all colors and shapes and sizes of them.

Her cell phone chirped as she pulled into her normal parking space at Valentine's. Sandy's name danced across the readout screen.

"Hey, there!" said Charlie into the speaker. "Working hard?"

Sandy's warm chuckle in her ear brought on an answering smile.

"Not as hard as I was a couple of hours ago. I've been baking all day, making desserts for Brother Bobby's homebound Christmas dinners."

Charlie chuckled as she pulled open the bar's back door and stepped into the kitchen. "He caught up with you, too, did he? I just dropped off some boxes of roast turkey slices."

"Well, I made Justin a deal. If he went with Ricky to take my pies to the church, I'd make another pie for dessert tonight, but then I realized I'm out of lemon so I can't make his favorite. And for some reason— Hang on a sec." The muffled sounds of toddler-speak came over the wire followed by Bethany's giggles.

So Justin *had* been with Ricky. Had Ricky deliberately tried to keep her from chatting with her old friend? That made no sense.

"Hello?"

"I'm still here."

"For some reason, I can't get through to Ricky's cell, so they're probably on the way home and in a dead zone."

"It's too bad Ricky isn't working today. I could whip up a pie and send it home with him." Charlie opened her locker and shoved her purse inside, then drew out the big white apron that was her kitchen uniform.

"Well, actually..." A nervous laugh accompanied the words. Uh-oh. Sandy was about to ask for something. "I was wondering if you might make one and come out here for Christmas Eve dinner. We're having lasagna, just family — if the guys get back from Cheyenne, that is. They've been delayed again."

Charlie's heart stuttered a beat. "Christmas Eve?" Anticipation stirred. She wouldn't have to be alone!

She entered the kitchen prep area to find it empty. Where was the new guy?

"Unless— Oh, dear..." Sandy's disappointment was tangible. "I never considered that you might already have plans."

"No... no plans. With the girls deciding to do their own things this year, I'm free." A sigh slipped out. What a thing to admit. "Actually, I was thinking of getting a kitten... you know, turn cat lady." And that was worse! What was wrong with her?

"Then you'll come for dinner?" pressed Sandy with new enthusiasm. "If the weather turns bad — and they're pretty sure it won't, according to the news — but if it does, you can always spend the night." Her tone took on even more animation. "In fact, spend the night anyway! You can bake your pie here and help me with breakfast Christmas morning."

"Oh, um..." Why not? "Well, would it be okay with..." ...*Justin?* "...the rest of your family?"

"Charlie!" Sandy huffed out a frustrated sigh. "You *are* family! So it's decided. You're coming."

Charlie hit the OFF button and stared at the phone lying in her palm. *What did I just agree to?*

The stainless steel doors leading into the bar swung inward to admit Bertie. "Oh, good, you're back. Luke was looking for you." She carried a tray filled with dirty dishes raised over one shoulder and gracefully swooped across the room. With little effort, she lowered the tray to the counter and began unloading it into the dishwasher.

"He probably wants to know why I'm late." Charlie walked toward the main bar.

"No." More dishes clattered into the racks. "He's handing out bonuses."

Perfect timing! She could shop for the McGees after work. If she ever figured out what to get Justin. That question had been plaguing her for weeks.

Chapter Three

Sandy surprised Justin by topping off his coffee before he could ask. Ah, the benefits of having a former bartender as a daughter-in-law. With quick and efficient movements, she stepped to the counter and slipped the pot back onto the warmer, then grabbed their plates.

As Sandy took her seat, Justin regarded the plate she'd set in front of him and sighed. Tex-Mex omelette made with egg whites and egg substitute, salsa and avocado, with a side of low-fat sausage and a whole bran English muffin. A nice "heart-healthy" breakfast. Ah... the side effects of having a former medical professional as a daughter-in-law. No bacon, no sodium, no fat. He rolled his eyes. And no flavor.

"So." Sandy added some salsa to her omelette then cut into the concoction with the side of her fork. "Charlie's car broke down."

Breakfast forgotten — mostly — Justin gazed up at his daughter-in-law. "Broke down? What's wrong with it?"

A blank stare rewarded him. "Um... it's broken down."

Justin snorted. "So you said. But what's *wrong* with it?"

In the middle of scooping a forkful of fake eggs — how did she eat that stuff? — Sandy faltered with her hand midway to her mouth. "It's... *broken*." She spoke slowly and carefully as she might to Bethany.

What? Am I three now?

"But broken how?" He concentrated on wiping the scowl from his forehead. "Like it doesn't start? Makes a noise? Won't go into gear? Has a flat tire?"

She angled a quizzical glance at him. "Broken. I don't know what's wrong with it. I'm not a mechanic."

"Well, why did you bring it up, then?" Justin picked up his knife and fork and cut into the omelette.

"Because she was going to deliver the Christmas dinner boxes to the homebound this afternoon." A sunny smile lit up Sandy's face. "And now she has no car, so she needs help."

Well, that sounded easy, and he was always willing to help a friend. "Sure, what does she need? Help fixing her car? Or is she looking for a new one?"

The smile turned smug. "Help delivering the dinner boxes. I volunteered you and Ricky after he gets home from school."

No way had he heard right. But as Sandy continued to smile, reality hit, and Justin stopped chewing. He swallowed the mouthful and gulped a splash of coffee. The cup settled back on the saucer with a clatter. "Beg pardon?"

"I volunteered you and Ricky to help Charlie deliver the meals from the church."

Dang it! He and the boy had last minute things to do. And delivering meals was going to put a crimp on the timing.

"When are Sean and Ryan due in?" If they got in early enough, maybe they wouldn't be too tuckered to help Charlie.

The smile drifted into a troubled expression. "Ryan called last night. They've been delayed again."

"Delayed?" His radar piqued. "What kind of delay? I thought they were just meeting with the auctioneer about putting up some bulls."

Sandy lifted a shoulder. "He didn't really have time to explain. They're leaving tomorrow first thing in the morning."

"Tomorrow's Christmas Eve," pointed out Justin. What in Sam Hill had his boys been thinking, even making a trip so close to the holiday? As far as he could tell, they could have handled the auction business over the phone or on the Internet — if it even had to be settled before the first of the year.

"Oh, yes. Don't I know that." Sandy's chuckle was a little forced. "What can I say? It must be something important." She stabbed the last bit of omelette on her plate, shoved it into her mouth, and then stood. "Excuse me. I have to get Bethany up."

With a clatter and a lot of stomping, the back door pushed itself open and a pint-sized tow-headed tornado whipped across the room on a beeline for Justin, bringing the winter chill with him. "Peepaw! Peepaw!"

"Well, hello there, Mitchell Mustang!"

The seventeen-month-old squirmed into his arms.

"Mitchell, you need to take off those muddy boots!" Melanie trudged in from the mudroom, carrying a gigantic blue and brown diaper bag and pulling a black overnight suitcase on wheels behind her. She smiled at Justin. "Hi, Dad. We're here."

Justin extracted his neck from the clutches of his grandson and cocked an eyebrow at his other daughter-in-law. "I can see that. And not that I mind — I love having my family around — but... why the luggage?"

"Sean said you invited us for Christmas."

He had? Justin blinked away his surprise. Was he going senile now? Losing what was left of his mind?

Mitchell stood on his toes and grabbed the last half of English muffin. With a crafty smile he held it up and pointed at the jar of grape jelly. "Jelwy?"

The diaper bag fell to the floor with a thunk as Mel dropped it and rushed toward the table. "Mitchell, don't eat Granddad's breakfast."

"That's okay. I'm finished." Justin waved her off and reached for the jelly jar. "Okay, young'un, jelly it is."

Sandy returned carrying just over two-year-old Bethany. "Oh, look, Bethy! Aunt Mel and Mitchell are here."

The little girl with the dark curls, so like her mom's, rubbed her eyes tiredly and stared. A giant grin widened her pouty lips and she struggled until Sandy set her down.

Mitchell handed off his jellied muffin, and the toddlers began a conversation in utterly unintelligible toddler-speech. Justin shrugged. As long as they understood each other...

Gesturing toward Mel's bags, Sandy grinned. "I have Sean's old room set up for you."

Alarm whipped through Justin. Even Sandy knew they had expected guests? *Was* he losing his mind? Had his heart attack the previous spring left him a mental case?

"Thanks!" Mel grinned and collected the diaper bag from the floor. "If you'll keep an eye on Monster Mitchell for a second, I'll get our luggage out of the way."

After she left, Justin stared at his plate in silence.

Sandy settled Bethany in her highchair then walked to the refrigerator. "I hope it's okay I invited Sean and Mel for Christmas." She poured two sipper glasses of juice and returned the carton to the fridge. "I thought it would be nice for the kids to be together for all the fun."

So... he hadn't invited them. Which meant he wasn't losing his mind. He sighed with relief. Good to know.

"Now, Ricky only has a half day of school, so he'll be home by eleven."

Bethany took the juice, but Mitchell shook his head.

With a smile, Sandy set the glass on the table and began scrambling some eggs — real ones that probably had texture and flavor. "Charlie has the next few days off, so she's at home waiting for y'all to pick her up. Don't be late getting home this time." She looked over her shoulder and pinned him in her gaze. "Oh, and I invited Charlie for Christmas Eve dinner, but since she doesn't have a car, I suppose she won't be able to come." Her lips lifted into a crafty smile. "Unless you can convince her to ride home with you tonight and she can just stay."

"Charlie?" His heart bumped up a notch even as his gut twisted. It was one thing meeting her casually around town or when he stopped in at Valentine's with one of his boys. But having her as a guest in his home? That was another can of worms altogether. A can he'd just as soon leave closed for a bit longer. "Ah... she probably won't want to come out—"

"Well, find a way to convince her," Sandy said sharply. She split an English muffin and dropped the halves into the toaster. In a softer voice, she added, "She's all alone this year. Her girls aren't coming."

All the bluster left him. Alone? He'd just assumed Charlie's family would come home, or at least one out of the three girls. His hand shook as he finished off his coffee. What would he do without his family? Sure, Charlie *lived* alone, and she was probably used to it. Well, maybe. But alone on the holiday...? No, Sandy had the right idea. He had to convince Charlie to come out to the Cross MC for Christmas.

And once he did that, he had a few calls to make.

* * *

"Finished!" announced Charlie as Justin climbed into the cab of Ryan's pickup after delivering the last box.

"You sure?" he asked as Ricky drove the vehicle forward. "That seemed to go fast."

"Maybe it was the company," teased Charlie, leaning back. Quickly, she buckled her seatbelt. They had completed the task in record time. It was barely dusk. And she wasn't quite ready to part company. "It's early yet. Do you want to stop at Valentine's? I just made some pecan pie. Or... lemon meringue?"

She knew he wasn't supposed to load up on the sweets, but old habits died hard, and she'd been indoctrinated from childhood to feed up her man.

Her man? Where had *that* thought come from?

"I could do with a slice of pie," he said, and his voice actually sounded... friendly again. Well, less gruff, at least. "If we can buy Ricky's silence, that is."

"What's in it for me?"

Oh, how much of a McGee he was, despite the unfortunate circumstances of his birth. Justin knew it, too. He literally beamed at the boy.

Ricky turned off the side street and headed through the center of town. As they passed City Hall, an amazing array of lights illuminated the building and grounds.

"Goodness, that must be what Henky was talking about at lunch today," exclaimed Charlie. "I haven't seen that old place so lit up in years... decades, actually. Remember back in high school, Justin? When a bunch of us went out caroling, and we carried strings of lights for the houses that didn't have decorations?"

Twin lines furrowed Justin's brow. "Umm-hmm... vaguely."

"Henky says Mayor Kelly didn't order extra decorations this year so no one knows who put them up." And Charlie had been wracking her brain since lunch trying to figure it out. "It's driving people crazy, but it's kind of cool to see folks having fun like we used to."

"Look at that," said Ricky, pointing at the church across from Valentine's.

A large manger scene had been erected in front of the church.

"What do you know?" Justin chuckled. "Brother Bobby's sure getting into the spirit."

"That just turned up there last night," said Charlie. "It was just out there when I left work. I never even saw anyone putting it up." And it hadn't been there that morning when she'd dropped off bolts of fabric and two brand new sewing machines for the Christian Ladies Quilting Club. She shrugged. "Pretty, isn't it?"

Ricky brought the truck to a stop in front of Valentine's. For being a couple of days before Christmas, it sure was hopping. Luke Corbett had worked hard to keep the changes Sandy had implemented while injecting his own brand of new life into Valentine's. He'd added some arcade games in the billiards area and opened the stage on Thursday nights for amateur entertainment. He'd brought in another cook to cover nights, a friend from his police force days on the East Coast who'd worked in food service. The timing had been perfect, since Charlie had wanted to cut back her hours. There just came a time a body needed to call it quits and go home for a long soak after a hard day.

Music blasting from the jukebox thumped, the vibrations rattling her teeth as they approached the door. It was a bit of a relief to make it into the kitchen away from the bulk of the noise.

"You listen to that all day?" asked Justin, setting his Stetson on the counter.

"It's somewhat quieter for the lunch crowd," answered Charlie. She nodded to the new cook standing at the prep island, where he was chopping onions. "Hi, Steve. We're just here for some pie. Mind if we eat it back here?"

Steve Phillips held up a finger. With his other hand, he worked a blue foam earplug from his right ear. "What was that?"

Justin snorted, and Charlie shot him a quelling glance as she explained to Steve what had brought them in.

"No can do, Ms. Charlie." Steve shook his head and spread his hands. "Your pies don't last more'n a couple hours. Luke just had the last piece of lemon meringue with his dinner."

What was that old saying? Best laid plans? She shot a wry smile at Justin. "Sorry."

"No problem." He shrugged. "We'll go by your place and pick up your suitcase then head back to the ranch." He sent her a slow wink. "I'm pretty sure Sandy'll give you kitchen time if you're inclined to bake us up a few pies. I sure do love your lemon meringue."

Pick up my...? "Excuse me... pick up my *suitcase?*" What the devil was he talking about?

One bushy, steel-gray eyebrow rose. "Sandy told me you were coming out to the Cross MC for the holidays."

Oh, that. "Well, that had been the plan, and she did ask me to do some baking," she admitted slowly, shaking her head. "But without a car..."

"That's not a problem." Justin glanced at Ricky. "We'll take you back with us. Tonight."

"Now? Oh, but I don't want to put anyone out..." Besides, she wasn't even packed.

Justin expelled a frustrated sigh. "Charlie, I've been hankering for one of your pies for weeks now. Sandy's good, but she's not you. Now, you promised me a piece of pie today, and it looks like I'm not getting one. Again." He shook his head and shot her a grin that took her back years, back to when life was less complicated. "So, if you want to talk about putting someone out, consider how long I've had a taste for one of Charlie Hains' lemon meringue pies. *That's* putting me out. Now, if you come out to the ranch with me, I figure by tomorrow at the latest, I'll have me some pie."

"It's only one day early, Ms. Charlie," Ricky pointed out with an engaging smile. "You don't *have* to come back with us tonight." He lifted one shoulder. "But you know Sandy'll just send us in to pick you up anyway."

She considered the evening she'd had planned for all of five seconds. A hot soak with a nice historical romance and then bed. It probably wouldn't be nearly as relaxing out at the ranch.

But it would be a lot more exciting.

And a lot less lonely.

A smile pulled her lips upward, and she shrugged. "Okay. Take me home so I can pack."

The only fly in the ointment was her lack of a present for Justin. Everyone else... but ideas for him remained elusive.

Chapter Four

The heady aroma of cowboy-strong coffee tickled Charlie's nose, and she inhaled deeply as she opened her eyes and took stock of her surroundings.

Diffuse light poured through a wide gap in the red tartan draperies covering the window. A matching comforter had kept her nice and toasty all night. As tempting as it was to linger in the softness and warmth, that coffee was calling her name. She pushed aside the quilt and sat, swinging her legs off the pillow-top mattress. It had to be fairly late if it was light already. Her fuzzy pink slippers were next to the bed, exactly where she'd left them the night before, and she slipped them on. The plush tan rug would keep the chill of the plank floor away, but the slippers would add an extra layer.

She hadn't slept so well in an age. Ricky had a nice bedroom, though playing poker with Sandy and Mel the evening before had been so much fun, she'd gladly have stayed on the living room sofa. But Ricky had insisted on giving up his bed while he took the converted attic bedroom. Charlie smiled and hoped he'd been as comfortable as she had been.

Standing, she reached over her head and stretched, breathing in deeply. An errant draft raised goose bumps that had her reaching for her blue velour bathrobe. The coffee smell grew, enticing her to find her way downstairs.

But first a stop at the window to check out the view.

She pulled the drape back and gasped. Puffy flakes of snow drifted down from a heavy sky. At least three inches lay on the ground already — enough to cover the grass and bow the branches of the jack pine in the front yard.

"Good gravy." She dropped the drape with a shiver. The storm that was supposed to track to the north apparently hadn't paid attention to the weather forecast.

A soft knock on the door startled her.

"Come in," she called, drawing her robe tighter.

The door pushed slowly inward, admitting Sandy, carrying a tray laden with a breakfast plate and, mercifully, a pot of coffee. Her face screwed up into a mock pout. "You're already up. I thought I'd surprise you with breakfast in bed."

Giggling self-consciously, Charlie tried to recall the last time she'd eaten breakfast off a tray in her room. Janet had already married and moved out, but Zoe and Heather had still been in high school, and they'd celebrated one Mother's Day by pampering her. And now they'd both graduated college.

She sighed. That long ago...

The smell from the tray tantalized, and memory of the bed's comfort had Charlie waffling. She hated causing extra work. Then again, Sandy had already brought the tray upstairs. Having her carry it back down so Charlie could eat in the kitchen would only be causing more work.

With a happy grin, Charlie hustled over to the bed. "I was going to ask if I can borrow your oven to bake Justin his pie this morning. Will you be using it?" She settled in bed and drew the covers up to her waist as Sandy extended the tray's legs and set it down over her lap. "What time does Justin get up?"

"I won't need the oven until I put the lasagna in to bake — probably about four o'clock. And I have a double oven anyway." With efficient movements, Sandy lifted the coffee carafe and poured the steaming liquid into the green and yellow coffee mug.

Charlie's mouth watered instantly.

"You take it sweet, right?" Sandy uncovered the sugar bowl and slid it closer. "Oh, and Justin and Ricky are already up and out of here on some mission."

Alarm sharpened Charlie's query. "Out, as in somewhere on the ranch? In this?"

"Actually, out as in they drove to Orson's Folly for some undisclosed reason." Sandy grimaced. "They were up at four, helping the new hand, Wade feed and check the stock so he could take off early to visit his parents in Riverton."

Charlie's appetite began to fade. "What in the hell is so all-fire important they have to drive in this mess?"

"Justin said it was important, and he wanted to get it done before the roads got too bad." Sandy shrugged. "Ricky's good behind the wheel, and he's used to driving in snow. They have their cell phones and the two-way. I really think they'll be all right. It's Ryan and Sean I'm concerned about."

"Have they left Cheyenne yet?" Charlie lifted the top off her covered dish and regained her appetite as the smell of short-stack pancakes and bacon wafted upward. "Maybe they should hold off."

"I haven't gotten an answer on their cells or on the motel room phone." Sandy's brow furrowed. "They aren't listed as checked out yet, so I have no idea why they aren't answering, but I hope it means they're at breakfast and they'll see the weather reports."

Shame inched into Charlie's consciousness. She'd been fretting over Justin being out in the storm, and he was only a handful of miles away compared to Ryan and Sean. Sandy was putting on a brave face when she must be worried out of her mind — a Wyoming blizzard was nothing to play around with.

A cup of warmed maple syrup sat next to her plate. Without another thought, she picked it up and bathed the hotcakes with sweet stickiness.

Coos and giggles arose from the baby monitor at Sandy's hip.

"And so the boss awakens." With a smile, Sandy walked to the door. "Come on down whenever you're ready. Looks like it's going to be an indoor play day, but maybe I can pick up on your pie-making secrets while Mel watches the kids."

* * *

The roads hadn't been too bad on the way in to town, and they'd made decent time. Ricky took his foot off the accelerator and slowed for the town speed limit. A slick patch in the road sent the pickup into a sideways skid. But with a flick of the wrist, Ricky expertly steered them back under control.

"Couldn't have done that better myself." Justin pushed his hat higher on his head and smiled. "Where'd you learn how to drive like that?" He was treading hot coals with any question he asked about the boy's past, but he also was a firm believer in not letting a past become a festering wound.

"Video games." Ricky flashed a grin.

So, that had been a relatively safe question. Justin eased out a breath and let his money ride on the next one. "Have you talked to your mom lately?"

Ricky gave a one-shoulder shrug as he slowed and made the turn into the tiny parking lot next to AJ's General Store. "She had finals in nursing school last week."

"Will you be seeing her over the holidays?" prodded Justin as he pushed open the truck door and stepped out, giving the boy time in case he needed a private reaction.

The door thunked gently closed fairly quickly, indicating no time had been needed.

"If the roads aren't too bad, I'm going up to Jackson a couple days after Christmas." Ricky caught up with Justin. "She doesn't... you know, she doesn't want to come back here."

That choice was understandable, given that the woman had lived such a hellish life. But it was a pity she and the boy had grown apart. Perhaps that was something he should work on for the New Year. Justin pulled open the door and stepped inside.

A newer country music trio blared a plea to "let it snow" over the speakers nestled in the ceiling. A snicker slipped out as Justin tugged off his deerskin gloves and rammed them into his pockets. He unbuttoned his jacket and reached into the inner pocket, snagging a folded sheet of paper and his reading glasses. He hated wearing the dang things, but it was one weakness he couldn't work around without appearing illiterate.

"Okay," he murmured, unfolding the paper as Ricky strode up next to him. "Take a look at this. Did we leave anyone out?"

Leaning over, Ricky perused the page filled with names and gift ideas. He tapped his employer's name. "You don't have anything next to Mr. Corbett."

Justin grunted. "Got that one covered. Seems the man has a strong liking for expensive cigars."

At first Ricky stared, then a sudden laugh bubbled up. "You're the one! You signed him up for Cigar of the Month Club!"

"Maybe." Justin scratched between his eyes then slid his glasses into place and looked over the list. "Walt likes to blast country music from that station down in Cheyenne."

"KDNC?" Ricky frowned. "How does he pull it in from so far away?"

"He got upgraded to a satellite subscription last year," admitted Justin with a shrug. What did it matter if the boy figured things out? After all, he was in on most of it at this point. "He needs a better sound system to go with it, though."

Together they wandered the aisles. Most of the shelves had been picked over but by some miracle they managed to secure gifts for everyone on the list as well as a selection of gift bags — Ricky's idea, since, as he pointed out, they had no time to wrap everything nice and neat.

They approached the portion of the store AJ reserved for miscellaneous pantry staples, and Justin paused. Charlie had brought along not only a suitcase but a grocery bag filled with gaily wrapped packages, and a crate filled with all manner of baking supplies. He sure hoped those supplies translated into pies. Lots and lots of Charlie's pies.

As they were moving off, his eyes fell on a box of Arm & Hammer. Ah, the memories that little orange-yellow box elicited. And those memories gave him an idea. He grabbed the box and dropped it into their cart.

"What do you need with baking soda?" asked Ricky, scrunching his face.

"Oh... you never know when some baking soda might come in handy." He started walking again.

"Fine, don't tell me," muttered the boy. "Hey, how come Ms. Charlie isn't on your list?"

"Got her covered, too," murmured Justin as his hand automatically drifted to the small, hard bulge in his right jeans pocket. Satisfied the red velvet box he'd been carrying around like a coward for the past two months was still there and safe, he smiled. And if that didn't work out, there was always the Jam of the Month Club certificate. "I think that's it. Do you have anything last-minute to pick up?"

Ricky started to shake his head, but then he hesitated, his forehead creased with a frown. "I never got anything for Natalie." He shrugged. "I know she's not coming, but I kinda want to have something for when she does get here."

"So you can guilt-trip her for not spending the holidays with us?" asked Justin, narrowing an assessing gaze on his youngest son.

"No! Geez, no!" Ricky exploded. He met and held Justin's gaze for a moment before he seemed to deflate. "I... I kind of want to have it for when she does come, so she doesn't feel like she doesn't count. Like if she didn't come, I didn't get her something. I just, well, kinda want it on hand so she knows she's important — whether she comes to visit now or later."

Whew! By the time the kid was done with his convoluted speech, Justin's head was spinning. "Well, okay, then." He shrugged. "What do you want to get her?"

Staring at his feet, Ricky dragged the toe of one boot along a line in the plank floor. "I saw these necklaces near the front of the store. Birthstones." He shrugged and looked up. "I thought since today's her birthday and all..."

"I think she'll like that, son. Let's go see what AJ has in that jewelry case of his."

Ricky was already off, calling over his shoulder. "There's a blue topaz in the shape of a butterfly I've been looking at."

Warmth spread over Justin as he watched his youngest boy make the purchase. Was he watching budding young love? Was it going to be reciprocated? Mel's baby was a few years more on the tender side than Ricky.

Shove it off, old man. Kid's gotta make his own choices. All you can do is make sure things don't get out of hand. He pushed their shopping basket to the checkout counter and began unloading it. His hand fell on the box of baking soda. Besides, he had his own romantic issues to be addressed.

They met out at the truck. A good inch had fallen during their foray into the store. They'd have to hurry and get the gifts delivered, or they risked being trapped between town and the ranch. A potentially deadly prospect in a blizzard.

"At least it's easy to sign the cards," groused Ricky.

Even with the heater blasting on full, Justin couldn't shake off the chill. So his normally spidery handwriting looked even worse than usual to his eye as he signed his tenth card. *Merry Christmas, from your Secret Santa.* Maybe he should have just gone with an abbreviated version, *Secret Santa*, but that seemed downright cold.

He popped the last card into the bag just as Ricky pulled into the first stop. Blackstone's Auto Repair. Getting the new sound system in unnoticed might have been tricky, since it was the largest of all the presents they'd picked up. But as luck had it, the tow truck was missing, which meant Walt was out on a call. Mission accomplished in under two minutes.

Luckily, the bulk of their stops fell along Main Street. Not only had it been recently plowed, but it was also on the way home. They weren't as lucky on their last stop as they had been on the first. The sheriff's four-wheel drive unit was parked out front of the office, indicating DC was in.

Pondering how to deliver the present, Justin picked up the green bag that contained a new digital camera. A man could never take too many pictures of a beautiful wife and daughter. But he wouldn't be taking any if he never got the camera.

"I got this," announced Ricky, lifting the bag from Justin's unresisting hands. Grinning, he jumped from the pickup and walked over to DC's SUV. After a glance over his shoulder, he tugged on the driver's side door, dropped the package inside, then closed the door again.

"I must be losing it." Justin shook his head. "Never thought about leaving it in his vehicle."

"I saw the lock wasn't set." Ricky shrugged. "Sometimes having a juvie record pays off." He put the pickup in gear and they cruised out of the parking lot.

The drive to the Cross MC was going to take a bit longer than the drive to town had. But that didn't mean they couldn't have a little fun. Justin pointed at the athletic field parking lot. It was empty but some contractor had recently plowed it. "Pull in here." He slid his boy a grin. "Those video games ever teach you how to spin a good donut?"

Chapter Five

Four pies sat cooling on the kitchen counter, two pecan and two lemon meringue. They made a nice complement to the apple and pumpkin pies Sandy had baked before Charlie had even gotten out of bed. The happy sounds of children laughing drifted in from the sitting room. The days of Charlie's young motherhood were long past, but they hadn't happened so long ago that her heart didn't flutter at some of her best memories.

She stepped into the mudroom and up to the back door to peer out through the window. Flakes that had tumbled lazily down earlier now fell at a straight slant, no longer fluffy but powdery. The kind of snow that built up quickly. How bad were the roads?

Not that it mattered. Justin and Ricky would be home when they got there. Same with Ryan and Sean. Charlie quelled the urge to run to the front porch and will two sets of headlights to appear. If Sandy and Mel could exercise confident patience, so could she.

Except she'd never been patient.

"They'll probably be here any minute," said Sandy from the kitchen doorway.

With a gentle start, Charlie whirled about. "I know." She forced a smile. "It's just hard... knowing we've got four people out in this who should be home. Did you ever get through to Ryan?"

After the briefest shake of her head, Sandy pushed her own strained smile onto her lips. "I forgot to leave a message for him to call, and they checked out a few hours ago." Her voice caught, and she drew a shaky breath. "I just don't understand. It's not like him not to call, keep me updated."

As if on cue, the wall phone next to the back door rang. Sandy grabbed the receiver before the second ring finished.

"Hello?" Her face fell, and then her forehead creased. "Wait! What? How did *that* happen?" Her shoulders sagged, and she nodded. "Okay. But they're both all right?" More waiting. "Well, should I get Mel to come after— Okay, okay. He is?" Another nod. "Tell them to drive carefully." Still frowning, she set the receiver back in the cradle and tapped it with her forefinger.

"Did Ryan and Sean break down?" asked Charlie.

"No-o-o, not Ryan and Sean." She rolled her eyes. "And not broken down."

Justin! Overwhelming alarm sent Charlie's heart into a staccato rhythm. "Justin and Ricky? What happened? Are they okay? We should go and get them!"

"They were arrested..." murmured Sandy, walking to the kitchen sink and turning on the faucet. "For reckless driving resulting in an accident."

"They had an accident?" The rest of the words sank in. "*Arrested?* What for?"

Sandy splashed water on her face and turned off the faucet. "They were doing donuts in the Orson's Folly Athletic Field parking lot. DC happened along just as they drove into a snowbank. He arrested them and took them in to the office, but he's releasing them. Walt's taking them out to the field to get Ryan's truck pulled out. Then they will *carefully* drive home."

Fear became seething anger and took over Charlie's typical composure. "Oh, for Pete's sake! What was Ricky thinking? He could have killed them both!" When she saw that boy she'd give him what-for.

Sandy's lips twitched. "Justin was driving. *Justin* was showing *Ricky* how to do donuts." A giggle slipped out and she slapped a hand over her mouth. "Or I guess how *not* to do them."

Charlie's jaw dropped.

* * *

Justin waited until Ricky scrambled from Walt's tow truck before he followed suit. The drop to the ground wasn't quite bone-jarring, so he shook it off and turned back around.

"Thanks for the lift, Walt."

"No problem. I had a run out Colt Ford's way anyhow." He grimaced. "Hey, sorry we couldn't get your truck out of that drift. I'll take Rayme out with the big rig day after Christmas and winch it out for you."

"Just give me a call, and let me know how much I owe, and I'll get a check to ya." *If Ryan doesn't kill me beforehand.* He smiled and grabbed the last of his Christmas packages off the seat then closed the truck door, gave it two slaps with his palm, and stepped back.

A gust of freezing air sent a snowy whirlwind dancing across the yard as Walt lowered the blade on the front of his truck and plowed a second swath to match the first he'd cut on their way in.

More wind whipped, and Justin eyed the heavy sky. "Looks like we're in for a lot more of this stuff before it's through."

"Yeah..." Ricky shot him a sideways glance. "What are you gonna tell Ryan about his truck? You know he's gonna be pissed."

"Well, if DC hadn't seen fit to call out here, I might have been able to tell him it broke down." He fixed his youngest in his gaze. "Not that I'm advocating you ever lie about such things, you understand."

"No!" said Ricky quickly, maybe a bit too quickly. Ah, well, he was a kid, and bound to make a few kid-type mistakes before he finished growing up.

The house door burst open, and Sandy and Charlie stepped onto the porch. "Time to face the music," he mumbled, pushing a smile onto his face. "Hey, got some nasty weather here, don't we? Anyone seen to the cattle yet?"

"Justin McGee, where is my husband's truck?" asked Sandy, planting her hands on her hips.

"Ahhh, well, funny thing happened..." He hedged. "We, ah, tried, Walt did, but..."

Charlie tucked her chin and raised her eyebrows, pinning him in one of *those* glares that let him know she'd hear the whole truth and nothing but.

"It's still stuck at the athletic field," blurted Ricky, caving in to the glare.

A sheepish grin wouldn't be held back, so Justin merely shrugged. "About those cows... the kid and I'll go check on 'em now."

"I'll go with," announced Mel, coming to stand in the doorway, bundled from head to toe. "Then Ricky can come help me check on Sean's horses."

A sigh of relief whooshed from deep in Justin's chest. *That a girl, Mel.* She always had covered his back. He stepped inside to drop off his package and change into work clothes.

Twenty minutes — and several pointed looks from both Sandy and Charlie — later, Justin eased out the back door to join Ricky and Mel.

"What were you *thinking*?" Mel ranted as they tromped three abreast across the yard to the cattle pens.

Well, so much for having his back. Over her head, Justin rolled his eyes at Ricky, who smirked and turned away.

The snow fences that lined the road by the pasture had done a decent job of keeping the track clear, at least for a little ways. They would be able to lay out some hay for the cattle, though they'd likely have to back the truck all the way to the stockyard.

"You drive, Mel, and I'll pitch the hay," suggested Ricky. "Dad, can you ride shotgun and watch for downer cows?"

Knowing it was useless to argue against being relegated to light duty, even if he did feel like he could at least drive, Justin merely nodded. "When the snow stops, someone'll have to take a couple of snowmobiles out. Ryan and Sean oughta be home by then."

Mel's lips thinned into a tense line as she rolled them inward. Her brow drew together, but she said nothing as she climbed into the flatbed truck, pumped the gas pedal, and turned the ignition key. As the engine coughed into life, the gauge needles registered: fuel on full, oil pressure in the green, coolant temperature one step above frozen. No dash lights popped on. Looked like they were good to go.

Justin climbed into the passenger seat and laid a hand on her arm. "Hey... They're okay, you know. My boys. They're McGees, and they're tough. They'll be home soon, you watch."

"I wish I knew why they didn't call," she said softly, checking the rearview. As soon as Ricky gave her the thumbs-up that he was ready, she set the truck in gear.

* * *

With a blustery sigh, Charlie slammed her book closed and set it on the coffee table. "I should have gone along and helped." Sure, it had been years since she'd pitched hay, and she'd never done so in a blizzard, but she was still fit enough.

"They won't let him do too much," murmured Sandy, looking up from her laptop. "We all kind of look out for him... though I'm certain he knows it, and that's starting to get to him."

A wry smile worked its way onto Charlie's face. "No, the last thing Justin would want is to be babied. I think he'd rather be—" She shook her head, refusing to contemplate the end of her sentence.

In front of the crackling fire, Patch suddenly lifted his head, ears pricked.

Clomping and stomping drifted in from the kitchen along with chatter. Charlie jumped to her feet and raced behind the dog into the kitchen, ready to welcome Justin with a cup of cocoa or tea, or even a swig of his "medicinal Jack." Someone laughed. Good! If they were laughing, everything must have gone well.

She skidded to a stop when she nearly ran into a slender teenage girl who stood in the middle of the kitchen, shrugging out of a sky blue ski parka. As the girl tugged off the pink knit cap and shook her head, the overhead light flashed on pale blond hair.

"Natalie?" Goodness, the child was the spitting image of her mother.

"Hi, Ms. Charlie!" Abandoning her coat and hat on the floor, Natalie rushed across the room and flung herself into Charlie's arms as two dark shadows filled the doorway and solidified into Ryan and Sean. "It's so good to see you!" She drew back and looked over Charlie's shoulder. "Is Mel here? Sean said we're all staying here for Christmas."

"Oh, my!" said Sandy with a gasp as she entered from the hallway. "Mel's gonna be so happy! Are your parents here also?"

"No." Natalie shook her head. "We talked about it, and they agree I should get to know my... Mel." Her grin lit her heart-shaped face. "Daddy took Mom to Hawaii on a second honeymoon."

"Oh, how thrilling," murmured Charlie, though she couldn't imagine celebrating Christmas without snow.

"Well, we're happy to have you here." Sandy directed a hard stare at Ryan as he emerged coatless from the mudroom. "You didn't call this morning. I had no idea where you were, or what you were doing."

He shrugged. "Nattie's flight from Oklahoma City was changed at the last minute because of the storm. We had to meet the plane at two a.m., so I didn't have a chance to call before we left. We tried when we were under way, but the storm seems to be messing with the cell towers."

Shaking her head, Sandy sighed. "And when did you know you'd be picking Miss Nattie up and bringing her here?"

Ryan rubbed the back of his neck and shrugged. "A couple of weeks. She wanted to surprise Mel."

Jaw dropping, Sandy recoiled. "So what does that mean? You couldn't trust me with keeping a secret?" Then she launched herself into Ryan's arms and smothered him with kisses. "I missed you."

"How about me? Did you miss me, too?" asked Sean, grinning at her. He'd shucked his coat and hat, but white puffs of snow slid from his boots onto the kitchen floor.

Aiming a stare at the boots, Sandy pointed to the mop parked next to the back door. "Did I miss you tracking crud all over my floor? Or sneaking in and stealing my fresh-baked cookies? No. I do know someone who *might* have missed you... a little. But he's still napping." As Sean cracked a grin and took the mop to his puddles, Sandy looked up at Ryan. "How was the drive?"

Her husband shook his head. "Bad and getting worse. They've got the streets plowed pretty good in town, but the state road's almost impassable." He chuckled. "And some poor fool got himself stuck out at the athletic field. Dang truck's buried under so much snow, he'll be lucky the plow doesn't run into it."

"Oh... really?" Sandy caught Charlie's eye and offered a small facial shrug.

Well, Charlie certainly wasn't going to say anything. That was between Justin and Ryan. Though if she could be around to see the fireworks when they happened...

Natalie slid her gaze to Charlie and scrunched up her nose. "Is Ricky here? Or did he work today?"

"Ricky, Mel, and Justin are out dropping hay..." Charlie glanced at the sunburst-shaped copper kitchen clock that had hung over the kitchen sink for as long as she could remember. Two o'clock... "But they've been gone over an hour..." She lifted her gaze to meet Sandy's. "Is that normal?"

Sandy abused her lower lip for a few seconds then shook her head. "Not really. And the two-way they probably meant to take is right there." Pointing toward the kitchen counter, she offered a weak — and totally unbelievable — smile. "But they were going to check the horses at Sean and Mel's, too. Justin probably just went along with them."

Ryan and Sean exchanged inscrutable glances then wordlessly shuffled back into the mudroom, where they sat and pulled on work boots. From the looks on their faces, the storm must have grown even worse.

Near the door, Patched whined.

Charlie contemplated bargaining with God, but she couldn't seem to move beyond one word. *Please...*

Once they were bundled up, it was almost impossible to tell the McGee boys apart. Ryan — at least she thought it was Ryan — grabbed the two-way radio from the counter before they left. As the door slammed shut, Sandy glanced at the clock. Was she marking the time? Charlie's heart stuttered. *Please...*

"Okay," announced Sandy, crossing to the pantry. "I have lasagna to make. Bethany and Mitchell are napping, but they'll only be asleep another half hour, so if you could listen for them, Charlie?"

"Sure!" Anything to be doing something. Dared she wake the kids up so they could play? Probably not a good idea.

"How can I help?" asked Natalie, bending to pluck her coat and hat from the floor.

"Well, there's not much to do. You'll be staying in Ricky's room with Charlie, if that's okay with the two of you?"

"Of course!" Charlie smiled. "Gotta warn ya, though, my Henry used to complain something fierce about my snoring."

Nattie giggled. "My mom says I could sleep through a twister."

"Come on." Charlie pointed at the pink and black zebra print suitcase on wheels. "Let's take your bag up to the bedroom. Then you can just relax. I seem to remember you like reading. Did you bring a book?"

A shadow fell over Natalie's face. "I downloaded lots of new books, but I forgot to pack my tablet."

Charlie gave in to a smile. "Well, allow me to re-introduce you to the world of books the way I've always read them. The McGees have a pretty substantial library."

Chapter Six

The bitter winter wind followed Ricky as he jumped into the cab of the flatbed and slammed the door shut. "The bottom of the truck's resting on the snow. Even if we dig out the wheels, the truck's hung up."

"Oh! We were so close!" Mel leaned forward and laid her forehead against the steering wheel. "Why did I have to forget the two-way?"

"It's my fault," admitted Justin. "If I hadn't wanted to go with you to check on the horses, you could have taken a snowmobile."

He shivered against the chill still emanating off Ricky's ski parka. One thing was for certain. They couldn't remain in the truck and they couldn't hike to one of the homesteads. They were pretty much screwed. He squinted at the tree line and tried to judge which house they were closest to, but shook his head. Looked to him like it was about even. Five minutes' travel by horseback on a clear day. Too bad it wasn't a clear day and they didn't have a horse.

"The way's easier back to your place, Mel," said Ricky, shaking his head. "But..."

"Not a good idea," added Justin. "If Sandy gets nervous and sets out looking for us before we get to your place and call — if we *can* call, assuming the phone lines are still up..."

Mel lifted her head and peered through the windshield. "I've walked this road lots of times. I know the landmarks. I can go get a snowmobile."

"No!" said Justin and Ricky at the same time.

"Things look different in the snow," added Ricky.

"We have to stay together," said Justin.

"And freeze as soon as the truck runs out of gas and we no longer have heat." The storm punctuated Mel's words with a sustained gust of wind that reduced what visibility they'd had to less than a foot.

As if to fulfill her prophecy, the engine sputtered and died.

"What the hell?" Mel turned the ignition key, but the engine spun without even coming close to turning over. Kicking the gas pedal a couple of times then trying again only brought more ineffectual spinning.

Frowning, she squinted at the instrument panel. The fuel gauge needle sat below the E. "It says we're out of gas. I don't understand. It was full when we started out. Have we been out that long?"

Justin didn't think so, but in a blizzard nothing was as it seemed. He shook his head. "Maybe we hit something in the snow. It doesn't take much to rupture a gas tank sometimes."

"I suppose it doesn't matter what happened at this point." Mel sighed. "We have to *do* something."

"We walk," said Justin, though he was utterly uncertain he had the wherewithal to actually make it home. Suddenly, all the precautions he'd fought against, which his family had forced on him anyway, made a lot more sense. *If I make it out of this, I'll eat oatmeal every morning.* Exactly with whom he was bargaining, Justin refused to consider, since it at least bordered on blasphemy to attempt a deal with God — at least that was what his mom had always told him. "I don't want Sandy settin' out to look for us, getting lost herself."

"There's a rope in the back," said Ricky, jerking a thumb toward the back window. "We can tie ourselves together so we don't get separated."

Justin grunted. "More learning from video games?"

A bit of mirth danced in the boy's blue eyes as he leveled a stare on Justin. "School. Mr. Ford came in and did a demonstration on search and rescue last week."

"Remind me to thank Colt," said Justin. *If I make it through this.*

"Wait here while I get the rope. Stay in the shelter as long as you can." Ricky popped open the door. The wind grabbed it as he jumped out, but he managed to wrestle it closed. The temperature in the cab dropped by several degrees.

A minute later, Ricky climbed back into the cab, rope in hand. His teeth chattered so hard they made Justin's jaw hurt.

Scratch the oatmeal. The second he got home, he was telling Charlie that he had deep feelings for her. Either she returned them or she did not. But obviously life was too short — and likely to be cut shorter at any moment — to put off the important stuff.

A distant light cut through the wall of swirling white and flashed off the truck's windshield.

"What's that?" asked Justin, pointing out the window, just as the whine of a small engine filtered into the cab.

* * *

When Charlie led Bethany and Mitchell into the sitting room, she found Natalie curled up with a brown leather-bound book that looked like it had seen better days. Cracks criss-crossed the cover, and the paper had yellowed with age. But the girl turned the page without looking up, seeming completely caught up in the story.

"What are you reading, honey?" asked Charlie.

Natalie gasped and jerked, then looked up, eyes wide. "I didn't hear you come in."

"So I gathered. Must be a good book."

"It's an old journal." The aged leather flashed in the light as Natalie closed the cover and studied it. "Someone named Greta Orson McGee wrote it."

Interest piqued. "Boy, it's been a while since I've heard *that* name. Not since we studied local history in school." Charlie ushered the children closer to the fire, where she'd left a tray of crackers and juice.

Bethany accepted a cracker, which disappeared into her mouth in two bites. "Dand-du," she said belatedly, spitting a few crumbs with the word.

"Who *was* Greta Orson McGee?" asked Natalie.

"Oh, she was— Oops!"

Mitchell reached his wriggly fingers toward a bright red ornament, hanging on a low branch of the Christmas tree in the opposite corner from the fireplace. A cracker did nothing to distract him, though he took it and continued his quest to undecorate the tree. After Charlie offered about a dozen toys, a red fire engine finally caught his attention.

"Fur fruck!"

Oh, goodness, that didn't sound too good. Charlie shook her head. What had Natalie asked? Oh, right, about Greta McGee. Charlie smiled. "Well, her father was one of the founders of Orson's Folly, and she was married to... hmm... Justin's... great? Yeah, I think his great grandfather."

Natalie's eyes grew wider still. "Really? Keagan?"

"Yes! That's it."

"That's so cool!" The girl waved the journal in the air. "She wrote all about their romance!"

Natalie Carter never ceased to amaze Charlie. Every time she'd come for a visit, she revealed a new facet of herself. Her excitement over Greta's journal was tangible. And infectious. It was almost possible to forget about Justin, Mel, and Ricky being lost in a blizzard.

"Where does she start the story?"

"About the time she met Keagan. But there's this one part..." She thumbed through the pages "...that I've been reading. It's almost like what's happening right now. It's even from Christmastime..."

* * *

Greta Orson McGee
December 23, 1866

I had no idea where Keagan had gotten to, or why he was so late. The babe stirred within my belly. Did he — for I knew, somehow, I would bear Keagan a son — feel the hunger as terribly as I? Keagan was only supposed to be gone for a day's hunting. He'd looked quite grim the night before he left but seemed loathe to speak his thoughts.

But a woman's wiles — even a woman huge with child, or perhaps because of that — often work miracles, and I got him to share his concerns with me.

Immediately, I wished I had left him to it. For he had decided if he could not find ample game, he might have to slaughter Martha, our weakest milk cow. I wept until my throat hurt when he told me that. It hardly seems fair that such a gentle creature should become our food simply because she does not give as much milk as her sister Olive.

Three days have passed since he left. I'd eaten the last of the rabbit stew the first day he was gone, certain that he would return quickly after a successful hunt. Carrots and potatoes I'd laid up from the autumn harvest would sustain me for some time, but our stores would never last the winter, and in truth they were not very satisfying without meat.

The babe turned again, growing restless.

"Oh, Keagan, my love, please come soon, so we are still living when you get here." But no one was there to answer my whispers.

Still, I refused to entertain the notion of horrors that might have befallen him. He was alive because he needed to be. His child and I needed him so.

The wind whistled through the eaves overhead, drawing me to the window. I lifted the deerskin flap I'd hung there to keep the cold from seeping through the glass. Miniature cyclones of snow danced across the yard between the cabin and the barn. I was grateful I'd seen to the animals earlier and wouldn't have to go out there for a while yet. I had gathered a handful of eggs. But even the chickens were slowing in their laying lately.

In my heart I knew I was panicking for no reason. When my husband was with me, I had no fear of the future. I knew he would see to my needs. But while he was away, worry and fear held me in their terrible grip.

Loud thumping against the side of the cabin startled me and sent me scampering away from the window. It stopped suddenly but then picked up again. Not quite rhythmic, I thought it might be the wind, but I couldn't be certain. My gaze strayed to the rifle above the mantel. It should be loaded. With trembling hands, I put the bullets in the side gate the way my husband had shown me the previous summer. Though the noise had stopped again, I turned my rocking chair to face the door and sat with the rifle across my lap.

"Please," I whispered to God. "Please bring Keagan home soon."

* * *

A gust of wind sent icy pellets splattering against the window behind Charlie and she jumped. It took a second to regain her bearings. The children still played with the handful of toys she'd parked in front of them. Natalie was staring at her, mouth agape.

"Are you okay, Ms. Charlie?"

A nervous laugh seeped out. "Oh, yes. But that story had me caught up in it. I almost heard the thumping myself."

A squeal arose from the kitchen that drove Charlie to her feet. "What on earth?"

Then she did hear thumping. And clomping. And hearty male laughter. Relief washed over her. They must be home! Charlie started for the kitchen but paused at the sight of the children she'd been charged with watching.

"You go, Ms. Charlie," whispered Natalie. "I want to surprise Mel!"

Charlie didn't need a second invitation. She raced along the hallway to the rear of the house, slowing down and taking a half second to catch her breath before stepping through the arch into the kitchen.

Amid the crowd of stomping, chatting, laughing people who'd just dragged themselves in from outside, Justin leaned against the doorjamb, still clad in his down parka. His face was a bit pasty, and dark bags had formed beneath his eyes. She'd not seen him looking so haggard since his heart attack.

Oh, dear Lord, he hadn't had another, had he? Her hands furled themselves into fists, and the air stalled in her lungs as she braced herself for the worst. No, surely not. They wouldn't be leaving him to stand in the doorway if he had. She released her pent-up breath.

But why *were* they letting him stand in the doorway? Patch nuzzled his hand then gently grasped it in his teeth and tugged. At least one member of the family had good sense. Charlie stepped into the room, ready to order Justin to sit.

Sandy beat her to it. "Come on, Dad. Have a seat at the table and I'll set you up with something hot. Cocoa or tea?"

"Something sure smells good," said Ryan, waggling his eyebrows suggestively.

The rumble in Charlie's stomach reminded her that she'd skipped lunch. Baking lasagna filled the room with a spicy tomato-and-cheese aroma, and it smelled like they would have fresh-baked bread to go with it. Her mouth watered.

"Well, that's dinner and I just put it on, so it still has two and a half hours to go." Sandy filled a mug with boiling water from the teakettle as Justin shrugged out of his jacket and handed it off rather awkwardly to Ricky, who disappeared with it into the mudroom.

Why had he balled it up so oddly?

Mel took Justin by the arm and led him toward the chair. An irritated scowl pinched his brow but he remained unusually silent. He did, however, extract his arm from her grasp with a little tug.

Too much fussing! He hated being fussed over. Oh, dear. He probably felt like a helpless invalid, weak and ineffectual. *I can fix this.*

Charlie met Justin at the table and pointed at the chair. "Sit down, old man. Have you any idea how many gray hairs you added to my head?"

Mel gasped, but from the corner of her eye, Charlie caught Sandy's head shake in Mel's direction.

With a grunt, Justin plopped into the chair and angled a look up at Charlie. "Who the heck can tell with that two-tone job you've got going on? Don't you think it's about time your hair picks a color and sticks with it?"

A smile pulled at Charlie's lips. The pallor in Justin's cheeks was being replaced by a healthy ruddy glow, and his eyes sparked with life.

"Dad!" began Ryan, but again Sandy shook her head.

Charlie patted her salt-and-pepper bob. "Maybe I like having silver highlights."

Another grunt slipped past his lips. "Then a few more shouldn't hurt." He glanced over his shoulder. "I want cocoa with marshmallow and whipped cream — the real stuff, not that fat-free crap. And I want a double of Jack on the side to warm my bones."

No one moved.

"I'm not getting younger waiting," he grumbled.

His words seemed to spur his family into motion. Without argument, Sandy set up the cocoa, adding a couple of puffy white marshmallows and then spraying a measure of whipped cream into a swirl on top before placing it in front of Justin. Ryan set a tumbler with the required Jack Daniels next to the mug of hot chocolate.

"Wait! Is Mitchell still sleeping?" asked Mel suddenly. "He'll never go down at bedtime!"

Charlie hid her budding smile behind a deadpan expression. "Oh, yeah, the children. I left them in the living room playing." As Mel's face drained of color, Charlie added for good measure, "They've got the fire to keep them nice and warm."

"Oh, my—!" Horror spread over her features as she took off at a run for the sitting room.

Sean and Ryan chased behind her. Sending Charlie a knowing grin, Sandy followed a bit more slowly.

"Woman! What did you do?" Justin leaned forward and studied Charlie's face.

She offered a shrug. "Sean and Ryan came back with a little surprise for Mel."

"Surprise?" Suspicion drew two vertical lines between Justin's eyebrows. "What kind of surprise?"

"One that comes with a name." Charlie grabbed his double shot before he could and downed half of it. "A little slip of a thing named Natalie."

"What?" The word exploded from Ricky in the mudroom.

Heavens, Charlie hadn't even realized he was still in there. He emerged from the tiny room, holding one hand behind his back.

Suddenly he sucked a fast breath. When he spoke, his teeth were clenched. "Nattie came for Christmas?" A spasm of pain marred his face, and he sucked in another sharp breath.

"Ricky McGee, what in tarnation do you have behind your back?" snapped Charlie. "Did you get your hand stuck in a bear trap or something?"

His gaze flew to Justin.

After a resigned sigh, Justin downed the rest of his shot and gave the boy a nod. "Might as well show her."

With a sheepish shrug, Ricky pulled his hand from behind his back. A tiny golden kitten dangled from his fingers. The little mite squirmed in his grasp, catching the tip of his thumb with its needlelike claws. Then, adding insult and more injury, it sank its teeth into the webbing between his thumb and forefinger.

"Shit!" he yelled. "You little—"

"Oh, what a little sweetie!" Charlie's heart melted and she hurried across the room to rescue the kitten from Ricky's precarious clutches. The second she had two hands around the tiny feline, it curled into her palm and began purring. "Where's your mama, little one?"

"Ah… it's the runt," said Justin, regarding Charlie closely. "Its mom didn't seem inclined to keep feeding it. Her. Or him."

"Which is it?"

Examining the scratches on his fingers, Ricky shrugged. "We didn't check."

A gentle lift of the tail revealed the telltale signs of a male kitten. "It's a boy," announced Charlie, petting the baby between the ears. "Aren't you a little pumpkin, all bright and orange?"

Patch stared up at the kitten, tail moving back and forth in a slow wag.

"Sandy's not crazy about cats," murmured Justin. "I was gonna sneak it upstairs."

Charlie sighed, knowing the little baby had already wormed his way into her heart. "Can I have him? I've been thinking it's about time I got a cat." She'd well and truly taken on the role of cat lady.

Chapter Seven

The warmth of the fire beckoned Justin toward dreamland, but he fought to keep his eyes open. Nothing said *feeble old man* more than falling asleep during family gatherings. From his seat in the brown leather chair to one side of the fireplace, he had a good view of everyone in the room. Which was also everyone in the house. No way was he going to snore his way into infamy as the family patriarch who couldn't keep awake.

He shifted in his seat and reached toward the side table, snagging a chunk of cheese and a cracker from the plate Sandy had laid out. Not that he was particularly hungry. In fact, his stomach was giving him fits because the promise he'd made out in the snow to tell Charlie how he felt had begun to weigh on him.

Between the scene in the kitchen, when she'd changed the group's somber and worried mood, and then her fascination with the kitten, the right moment simply hadn't presented itself. He popped the cheese and cracker into his mouth and chewed. Not yet.

He glanced at the dog pillow in front of the hearth, where the little ball of orange Charlie had insisted would be called Punkin lay sprawled. Patch lay on the hard floor staring at the tiny thing that had appropriated his bed. Every so often his tail *thunked* the floor, though, and he licked the orange head between the ears, a signal he'd accepted the kitten as part of his life.

If only it were that easy.

Across the room, Charlie was sipping pretend tea from a toy teacup at Bethany's request. She handed the cup back to the toddler with a smile and murmured, "Thank you, my lady."

He'd seen that game before. His granddaughter could beguile the adults in her life into playing her games for hours, only releasing them from the spell when she fell asleep or developed a fascination for something else.

Or when someone else intervened. A smile crept onto Justin's face as Sandy joined the pair on the floor, holding out a candy cane. When Bethany reached for it, Sandy laughed and pulled it away.

"Ah-ah! You have to sit with Mommy to share one of these, remember?"

Seeming years younger than her age, Charlie scrambled to her feet and sauntered to the sofa. She grabbed a cracker on the way down. "Hey, Nattie, why don't you read some more from Greta's journal?"

Interest piqued, Justin scooted to the edge of his seat and turned his attention on Mel's daughter. "Greta's journal?"

Natalie held up an ancient leather-bound book. "This! I found it on your bookshelf. It's a journal written by someone named Greta Orson McGee. Ms. Charlie said she was your great grandmother."

"She... was." He shook his head. "But I didn't know we had one of her journals. What did she write about?" Exhaustion fled. But so did the desire to work at getting Charlie alone.

Showing a bit of shyness at first, Nattie opened the journal and flipped through the pages. "Greta was just sitting in the rocking chair with the rifle because of the thumping while she waited for Keagan."

Justin held up a hand. "Wait. Thumping?"

"It was the day before Christmas Eve, and she was waiting for Keagan to come home. He was out hunting, and he was late." As she caught him up, Charlie spoke with animation and hand gestures. Lots of hand gestures. He couldn't wrestle his gaze from their graceful movements through the air.

"Ahhh," said Justin with a nod. "It was a tree making the noise."

Charlie stopped talking and folded her arms across her chest. "Now, how on earth would you know that if you've never read her journal, old man?"

"I don't have to read her journal. I've been up at the old homestead," he said, shooting her an exaggerated eye-roll. "They built the cabin in the shade of a cottonwood."

"Hrumph, you're forgetting I've been up there, too." Charlie stood and planted her hands on her hips. "There is no tree anywhere near that old cabin."

All eyes turned toward Justin.

He stood as well. "But there *is* a stump." And he stalked across the room toward Charlie. "Gus and I found it when I was just a kid. It's hollow and we used to hide notes there for the ghosts."

Charlie narrowed her eyes. "You did n—"

"Wait, wait, wait!" Sean leapt up from his seat on the raised hearth. "What ghosts?"

"The ghosts in your father's head," grumbled Charlie, angling an exasperated glare at Justin.

"No, no, I've felt them, too," piped up Ryan. He stretched and slumped back in the leather chair, opposite the fireplace to the one Justin had been occupying. "Usually around summer solstice."

Sandy aimed a kick at her husband's foot, striking dead on the bottom. "You have ghosts and you never shared them with me?"

Ricky and Natalie exchanged grins as Ricky pointed to the ceiling.

"Mistletoe!" squeaked Nattie.

Following the direction of Ricky's gesture, Justin looked up. A healthy round sprig of green leaves and white berries hung directly over him and Charlie.

"Kissy time!" sang out Mel.

Soon the room was alive with a chorus of "Kiss! Kiss! Kiss!"

Pink bloomed in Charlie's cheeks then deepened to crimson. Oh, this was going to be fun. Justin leaned in a little.

The chanting intensified.

Or maybe it wouldn't. For all that he wanted a proper kiss, it wasn't going to happen with his children watching and critiquing his technique. With a grin and a wink at Charlie, he tilted his head and pressed a quick kiss to one soft cheek.

His heart and body joined hands and protested together as he backed up a step, but he squashed the pangs and tingles that would otherwise have spurred him on.

Something flashed in Charlie's eyes. It came and went so fast, Justin had no idea what to call it, but she hadn't been unaffected by the contact.

"Ghosts," he murmured. "They're everywhere out there." Then he strolled back to his seat, snagging a couple of cheese cubes and some grapes on the way. "But the thumping was a tree."

"Let's find out. Maybe she tells," suggested Nattie with a nervous giggle. Casting a glance at Ricky, she opened the journal and cleared her throat.

* * *

Greta Orson McGee

I came awake with a start. The rifle had slipped to the side but at least it hadn't dropped to the floor. I made haste to right it in case I had need of it. How long had I slept, sitting in that hard wooden rocking chair? And what had roused me? Darkness had fallen, but the fire hadn't yet died, thank goodness. I sat very still, listening for the slightest noise, but heard nothing.

Slowly, I stood, but it was awkward with my round belly and the rifle in my hand, and the movement brought on a sharp pain in my right side. A moan pushed up from my throat as I fell back into the chair. The pain eased some, but I could hardly stay in that rocking chair forever. So I rested the gun against the table next to me while I tried again to rise. Pressing a hand to my side, I got up as carefully as possible. This time the pain happened on the left side, and it was all I could do not to cry out. But at least I managed to get to my feet.

A whisper of a knock came at the cabin door. Had that been what had awakened me? What should I do? I knew it couldn't be my Keagan returning home, for he would have no reason to knock.

The soft rapping came again, along with more thumping on the side of the cabin. In my chest, my heart echoed the thudding, and in my belly, my babe fluttered.

Perhaps it *was* Keagan. If he were injured or ill, he might need assistance. My gaze flickered between the door and the rifle. If intruders waited outside, they surely wouldn't be knocking to request entry. They could easily break the lock and simply enter. I picked up the rifle and made certain it was ready to fire if I found I had a need to shoot. Then I walked to the door, held my breath, and lifted the latch.

Wind pushed the door right out of my hands and it slammed against the wall. I peered out into the darkness. At first I saw nothing, but then I heard a whimper. I followed the sound, certain I would find an animal, a dog or perhaps even a wolf.

But it was a small child. An Indian girl, one of the Cheyenne who sometimes passed through the area. They usually kept to themselves, and we to our own, and never had we so much as raised a word between us.

The child could be no more than seven or eight years. Wrapped head to toe in deerskin dress and buffalo fur cloak, she looked near frozen.

"Oh, sweet mercy." I stepped aside and gestured for her to come into the cabin.

But the child shook her head and instead disappeared into the swirling snow.

"Wait!" I cried, and stepped out into the frozen night.

I'd never felt anything so cold. It went all the way into my bones. I almost ran back inside, but the child had looked terrified, as though on some urgent mission.

So I followed her into the storm. She had gone around the side of the cabin from where the thumping had arisen. Shadows reached out to embrace me as I rounded the cabin's corner, and it took some moments before I could see. I made certain to hold onto the outside of our home, knowing if I strayed, I would be consumed by the blizzard and might never find my way back.

"Oh, dear Lord, please protect my husband," I whispered. For he was out in that nightmare, and I knew only a miracle from our merciful God would be able to save him from the teeth of the storm.

The wind, howling through the branches of the cottonwood under which we'd built our home, raised the hair on the back of my neck. It was there, at the base of that tree, I spotted the Cheyenne child. She was kneeling next to a figure that lay in the snow, nearly buried.

A woman, I saw instantly. Her long silvery hair had plastered itself against her face, hiding her features. She moved weakly but couldn't seem to stand. A gust of wind sent a shower of snow falling on all of us from the branches of the tree overhead.

A horrible thumping began, the same as that I'd heard from inside, only much louder. Startled, I looked up to see one of the lower branches had cracked and hung by a sliver. As the wind gusted, the loose branch banged against the cabin near the roof. The Cheyenne woman moaned. The cold was becoming painful against my wet clothing.

I leaned close to the woman. "Can you get up if I help you?" I tried to make the motions, hoping she could understand my intent. More sharp pains attacked me as I got my hands under her elbows and helped her to sit then to stand. She leaned heavily on me and tears sprang to my eyes as we struggled back around the cabin.

"Manda!" she called in a weak but frantic voice.

In an instant the child was at her side, and we all stumbled into the cabin. I helped her to the bed then quickly returned to the door and bolted it closed. The wind had nearly blown the dying fire out. I had to tend it before I could see to the old woman.

"I'm just going to stir up the fire," I said, not even knowing if my words were understood, but hoping my tone conveyed benevolence. As soon as the fire caught, I set about lighting a lamp. "There!" I turned, triumphant in my accomplishment and already feeling much warmer despite my wet clothing. "We'll have to get out of our wet things. I have some blankets that will keep..."

The woman sat on the edge of the bed. She'd thrown off her wet cloak and removed the child's as well. The little girl wore her hair in a long braid down her back. The woman's — was she her mother, perhaps? — hair fell in dark, damp waves about her shoulders.

"You're not old!" I blurted.

It must have been a trick of the light, or perhaps the covering of snow that had made her hair seem pale silver. For in truth she was not much more than my own age.

"My name... is Greta." I pressed my hand over my heart. "Greta."

"Greta," said my visitor slowly, as though testing the sound. She smiled and began to speak. Though her voice was hoarse, her tone was lyrical as she spoke in halting English. "I... am Asha." She pointed to the child. "My... daugh— daughter. Manda."

I handed her the blanket folded at the bottom of the bed. "You and Manda must get out of your wet things."

Asha startled me by suddenly reaching out with both hands and cradling my swollen belly. The intrusion was so abrupt, so unexpected, I had to force myself to stand still.

"Your child... he will come soon?"

"Yes," I murmured as the heat of embarrassment at such intimacy with a stranger rushed into my face. "Quite soon, I think." A nervous giggle slipped out.

"Your man... is... uhm... is near?" she asked, dropping her hands.

"Yes," I answered, probably a bit too sharply. "He... he went out hunting."

She frowned. Did she not understand?

"To get food?" I pretended to put food in my mouth and chewed.

Asha broke into laughter. "Yes... I understand. My man has been gone, uhm... many days. He also went in search of food."

"Oh." My face grew even hotter. "Your English is very good." Why had I said that? It sounded like an insult.

"I was taken from my family and... sent to a white man's... uhmm... boarding school. We were only... allowed to speak English."

"You were taken from your family?" Horror washed over me. I could only stare, even knowing how rude I was being. "Who would do that?"

She studied the floor. "Soldiers... came to our people... and said we must go. I was about Manda's age."

At the sound of her name, the little girl drew closer to her mother.

"A family took me in the year before I... ahhhm... became a woman?" She frowned then nodded. "You know... when I could bear a child."

As before, the intimacy of such a private conversation brought the heat of embarrassment. At this rate, I wouldn't have to change out of my wet clothing. My blushing would dry me from the inside out. "Yes," I finally managed to choke out. "I understand."

"I... had great *nóhtsevátsestá*... ahm... yearn... yearning in my..." She patted her chest "...in my heart for my home and *manáhestótse*... my family. So I re-returned. I learn — learned? — English but some words are still... uhmm... hard? Hard to say."

My mind reeled with possibilities. What if she were a fugitive? Wanted by the soldiers who had taken her? "Are you... are you in trouble?"

"No!" she said quickly, shaking her head, but her eyes were wide and fearful. "My man's... father had... *nésenovomóhtahe*... sick, very bad sick?"

I nodded but terror speared my heart. Had Asha brought sickness into our home? I touched my swollen stomach, afraid for my unborn child, as I tried to still my trembling. She appeared rather well in the dim light of the fire, considering she'd been outside and exposed to cold and snow. Still, I had to know.

"This sickness... is it... Do you have...?"

Compassion replaced her fear and she shook her head. "Ishaynishu... my man... his father was an elder. Very old and... it came to his end time."

The sharp pain that had been bothering me had gone but in its place, a dull ache had settled into my lower back. I rubbed at it, shivering against the cold, and realized I still wore my wet clothing. Quickly, I unfastened my dress and struggled to get it over my head. Gentle hands joined mine as Asha lifted the dress off me. She grabbed the wedding ring quilt that had been lying across my bed and wrapped me in it.

And so we sat, wrapped in blankets as the fire warmed the cabin, and Asha told me the rest of her story.

"The rest of our people had to leave... the cold was coming. But Ishaynishu's father cannot travel. *Mahta'sooma* had left him but not his *omotome*. We waited with him until... ahmm, until he left his body to walk the road to *Seana*."

"Your people left you behind?" I couldn't fathom the horror of an entire community simply moving away, abandoning a family because of an illness. When my father had passed, the people in the small town he'd founded had rallied around me, helped take care of me until Keagan decided he was in love with me.

Her smile was sad. "They had no other choice. Just as we had none."

"But... how did you come to be out in the storm? Surely you had shelter... a home?"

"After Ishaynishu went to hunt for food, there was ahm... fire." She spread her hands and the blanket fell from her thin shoulders. "From... cooking. I tried to follow where Ishaynishu hunts but... he is not there, he is nowhere, and then comes the storm."

I wrapped the blanket back around her. "You're safe here. I have a little food. Some flour and a few vegetables I put up. Some — eggs, and a little venison jerky."

Panic urged me to stop. I was offering the last of the food we had. We might starve without it. But Asha and

Manda were horribly thin. I could see they'd been eating poorly for quite some time.

Asha glanced at her child. "That is... Thank you. If you can just feed Manda, I will be—"

The air left me in a rush. This woman would die that her child might live. I shook my head and sent her what I hoped was a friendly smile. "We will *all* eat. And then we will trust that God will provide what we need next."

* * *

Natalie lowered the journal with a deep sigh and reached for her soda.

Charlie wanted to grab the book from the teenager's lap and read more, but she could hardly fault Natalie for wanting to break. "Wow, that's intense."

A snort came from across the room. "Told you the noise was a tree," said Justin, stretching his arms over his head.

"Well, it wasn't *just* a tree," Charlie fired back. "Asha and her daughter were out there."

He pointed a finger at Charlie and looked along his arm, eyebrows raised. "The *people* weren't making the thumping sounds."

"You don't know that, old man." Charlie narrowed one eye. "And stop pointing at me before I bite that finger."

A slow grin spread over Justin's face as if he was about to dare her to do just that. But he laced his fingers behind his neck anyway.

"Did Keagan make it home that night?" asked Mel from her cross-legged seat on the floor, where she sat handing Mitchell toy after toy.

"Give the girl time to recover. I'm sure she'll finish reading to us." Laughing, Sandy strode in from the hallway with a tray of drinks. When had she left? "I've got more soda, some iced tea but we're out of lemon, and the pot has cocoa. Sorry; we're saving the whipped cream for the pie."

Charlie stood and stretched, then walked over to the window and peered into the gloom. The wind still blustered, throwing ice pellets against the glass. A crusty sheen was forming on the snow outside. With a shiver, she dropped the curtain and hurried over to the fireplace.

Punkin rolled onto his back and bicycled his feet in the air. "We have no kitten food," she murmured, crouching and rubbing the tip of his nose.

Justin coughed the word "tuna" into his hand, earning a long intense stare from Sandy. He flashed a grin at his daughter-in-law and sent Charlie a wink.

A bit of melancholy settled in Charlie's heart. They were such a close-knit family. And she wasn't an outsider; the McGee family had welcomed her into the fold long ago. But golly, she missed her daughters... even more so than normal. All three would be just as caught up in Greta's story as she had been, but Zoe in particular. Zoe was her little romantic.

With a sigh, she straightened up and wandered to the drink tray to pour a cup of cocoa. Maybe Justin would like one, too. As she glanced over her shoulder, she was startled to discover him right behind her.

"Don't mind if I do." He reached around her and lifted the cup from her fingers with a chuckle. But then he bent, standing so close she could feel his body heat along her spine. Warm breath tickled her ear. "That was quite a sad sigh. Thinking about your girls?"

Oh, he did know her so well. No point in denying his insight.

"A little. And it's not that it's not really nice being here with all of you. It's just..." Because she was tempted to lean back against him, she stepped forward and chose another mug. "...this is the first year we've all been scattered for Christmas."

"Well, you never know what might happen. These things have a way of working out, don't they?" He nodded toward Natalie, who had opened the journal again and seemed to be ready to pick up the story.

"I tried calling them earlier, but none of them answered." She shrugged and pasted on what she hoped was a suitable unconcerned look. "I suppose they all have last-minute errands like anyone else."

The window rattled, and the lamp on the side table stuttered. Charlie held her breath. It could be an even longer night if the storm took out the electricity. But the flickering stopped and the light brightened the room once more.

"Okay, I'm ready to read some more," announced Natalie. She certainly seemed to be enjoying the limelight. "She skips ahead a little to the next day."

Chapter Eight

Greta Orson McGee
December 24, 1866

Sharp pain in my middle dragged me from slumber. At first I feared someone had stabbed me or even shot me.

But all was quiet in the cabin. Little Manda lay snuggled beneath the counterpane, snoring softly. The other side of the bed was empty, the coverlet folded back as though someone planned to return.

Asha! I twisted, scanning the room, seeking her. The fire had died but I could make out her silhouette. She prodded the embers with the poker and laid another log on top. Then she swung the kettle back over the hearth and turned.

As the fire flared to life, light flooded the room, and it took me a moment to realize that she had lit the oil lamp.

"We need the warmth and the light to welcome your child," she murmured, smiling as she approached the bed.

"To welcome my...? I don't understa—"

Hot agony started in my back and squeezed around to my belly. To my mortification, I couldn't stop the moan that tore from my throat.

Asha was at my side in an instant. She took my hands and stooped down in front of me. "You must breathe slowly and deeply." A wince marred her face, and she gasped.

When I looked down, I realized I was squeezing her hands so tightly, it was a wonder I hadn't broken her fingers. I tried to release her, but it was as though my hands had frozen in place.

"Mama?" Manda scrambled to her feet.

Asha spoke to her daughter in their language, and Manda jumped out of the bed. As my pain subsided, Asha reclaimed her hands and touched me on the shoulders, rubbing gently. "I can help you through this. I have given birth two times, and I have... uhm... assisted many woman — women."

"Twice?" I looked at her little girl. "But... where?"

A shadow of sorrow fell across her face. "Manda is my youngest child. Honiahaka, my son, went with his father on the hunt."

The hunt! Her words reminded me that my own husband was out somewhere hunting.

"I can't have my baby now," I insisted as another dull ache began in my back. "My husband— I don't know where he is, if he's— hurt or— if something is wrong." Tormenting pressure encircled me. Asha demonstrated how to breathe by drawing deep breaths then blowing out, but my ability to even pull in air was gone.

Tears streamed from my eyes, soaking my cheeks and then my nightgown as the pain subsided. I pushed to my feet and stumbled across the small space from the bed to the window. Surely I would pull back the deerskin and see Keagan heading across the yard.

A blast of cold slapped my face through the windowpane. A shiver raced through me as I wiped the glass and peered outside. A brilliant round moon hung low in the sky, its silvery light gleaming off the snow on the ground and sparkling off the ice coating the trees. It was the middle of the night, yet it was nearly as bright as day.

"The storm stopped," I murmured, for the first time realizing no wind howled through the eaves. "Keagan will find his way home now."

"The air grows colder," warned Asha, slipping the deerskin curtain from my hand and laying it against the window again.

"He can come home now, so I can wait to have the baby."

A slow chuckle issued from Asha's throat. "Your... baby might have another idea."

"Oh, no, I can rest, and—" The pressure gripped me again, even harder than before. "I need — to lie — down," I said between gasps.

As Asha assisted me to the bed, a gush of warm liquid burst from inside me and cascaded down my legs. I bit back a cry of distress as Asha only smiled and nodded.

"Your baby has a... different plan, Greta."

Time was lost to me as everything blurred together in a whirl of pain and exhaustion. Asha tended me, reassuring me with soft words, sometimes in my language and sometimes in hers. It didn't matter. Even when she spoke English, I didn't know what she was saying.

Excruciating tightness squeezed me in the middle, and a scream burst from my throat before I could stop it.

"Soon," murmured Asha. "You will hold your little one soon."

She began to sing in deep, honeyed tones, her voice rising and falling, and somehow the rhythm soothed me in between bouts of searing agony. Surely I would be ripped apart bringing my child into the world.

"This time, when the pain comes, you must push," she said from between my legs.

The heaviness built and my breath stalled in my lungs. I struggled to do what she asked, but my attempt was pitifully weak. I was so exhausted. Then another voice joined Asha's, and when I glanced to the side, Manda sat cross-legged on the floor singing along with her mother.

"What... what is that song?" I asked.

"A simple *vávaóestovohe*... ahmm, a lulling song?"

"A lullaby?" The sweet peacefulness of the song suddenly made sense.

"Yes... but a special one. Uhmm, *osáane* — be-begin, a beginning song. We are singing your child's *omotome,* the gift of breath, and his *mahta'sooma,* his spirit, into the world," murmured Asha as she wiped my face with a cool cloth. "His spirit."

"Manda has a — beautiful — voice," I whispered, dropping my head back on my pillow.

A smile filled with pride slipped over Asha's face. "In your, umm… language, her name means Harmony."

Viselike pressure squeezed my belly again, followed by a scorching sensation between my legs. The moment I stiffened, Asha moved to the foot of the bed again.

"You must push now," she said with urgency that gave me strength. "Hard."

Manda's voice faltered, but Asha picked up the song and soon Manda joined her again. In anguish from the burning, tearing feeling, I could not stop my screams from overwhelming their beautiful music.

When the cabin door exploded inward, Manda's song became a scream as she raced to hide behind her mother. A crazed man stood on the threshold, his gaze flashing wildly around the room and lighting on me.

With blessed relief, the pressure squeezing me suddenly eased and the baby slid from my body. Asha continued to sing. I couldn't see her but I sensed her moving as I lay back, spent, and struggled to catch my breath.

"What the hell?" growled Keagan, dropping his rifle and the dead buck he carried from his shoulders. In seconds he strode across the floor, looking like he intended to harm Asha.

"Keagan!" I shouted weakly, unable to do more than lift my hand in his direction. "I'm not harmed. This is Asha. I'm having our child now." Between wheezing breaths, I struggled to get the words out around my thickened tongue.

"You are not having your baby," said Asha, looking up with a smile. Calmly, she held up a pale, wet infant. "You have had your son."

The baby's face crumpled and he began to whimper, weakly at first but Asha started singing again, and soon her voice was joined by my babe's lusty cries.

A whoosh of air left Keagan as he stared at our son, and then he visibly relaxed and took a step forward. "He's loud," was all he said as he kept his gaze fastened on the baby.

"He howls like a… ahhmmm, a *ho'néhéškéso,* ahmm, wolf pup."

A shadow darkened the doorway behind him. My heart leapt into my throat. A weak cry slipped past my lips, and I raised my hand to point, but my husband was focused on our child.

Joyful cries rose from Asha and Manda, and the little girl scrambled across the room. The shadow drew apart and became two people, a Cheyenne man and a boy who could only be his son.

"This is my man, Ishaynishu," said Asha, nodding at the man, who was lifting Manda into the air, a smile on his face. "And our son, Honiahaka."

"We found each other when we were hunting," explained Keagan, motioning for the two Cheyenne to enter the cabin. Once they were inside, he closed the door behind them. "When we went to their camp to seek shelter, the tipi had been burned. Ishaynishu feared harm had come to his family, but we tracked them here."

The boy carried two fat turkeys by their legs, one in each hand. Black feathers fluttered as he laid the dead birds next to the deer my husband had dropped on the floor.

I met Asha's eyes. "God provided," I whispered.

And he had brought our families back to us.

* * *

Natalie closed the journal with a sigh. "Their baby had the same birthday as me."

A chill blasted through Justin, and he quickly sought out Mel. Tears streaked over cheeks that looked far too pale. She stumbled to her feet and thrust Mitchell into Sean's arms, then headed for the hallway.

"Excuse me," she murmured quickly.

Natalie's eyes widened at her mother's sudden departure, and her hand flew to her mouth. "What did I do?"

"Nothing!" said Charlie fiercely, jumping up from her seat and rushing to the girl's side. "It's not you, honey."

Sandy extricated herself from under Bethany and stood, taking a few steps to follow Mel.

"Sit down," growled Justin, pushing to his feet. Confound it, his old bones made moving tricky as hell. He cast Charlie a smile and a wink, then mouthed "five minutes" as he passed her and walked into the hallway.

Mel hadn't gone far. She sat on the third step of the staircase leading to the second floor. Light from the lamp on the foyer side table lent her pale blond hair a golden glow.

"You look like an angel," murmured Justin as he approached.

Tear tracks glistened on her cheeks as she lifted her face. "A pretty pathetic excuse for an angel, huh?"

His lips tugged upward as he chuckled. "Naw... just pretty. You okay?"

"I was wishing I'd had an Asha to sing my baby into the world." With her fingertips, she wiped the moisture from first one eye then the other. "Someone to save her, to stop my father from putting her in a garbage can at a freeway rest stop."

"Well, first off, start by recognizing that Nick DeVayne was a lot of things, and jackass is right at the top of that list." Justin scratched his jaw. "But that man was never your father. Not in the real sense."

Shaking her head, Mel lowered her gaze. "It doesn't really matter what you call him. I didn't protect my baby. And there she is, sitting in there reading about another baby born years before on her birthday, and she sounded so happy, like it was a connection somehow."

He offered a facial shrug. "It is a connection. All of life has connections. Circles. She found one of her circles when she met you is all. You're connected here through Sean, and that gives Natalie a connection as well."

"I should have done better by her." When Mel looked up again, more tears had welled in her eyes. "I failed her."

"Failed who?" came Natalie's sharp voice from the living room doorway. "Me? I never felt like anyone failed me! Especially not you!"

"Nattie!" Mel jumped to her feet, scrubbing her eyes. "I'm sorry! I didn't mean to be such a Debbie Downer. I just got emotional when I realized this is your birthday." She offered a shaky grin. "You know, I didn't get you any—"

"Yeah, you did, Mel!" said Ricky, entering the hallway on Natalie's heels. "Don't you remember? You asked me to stash it here. I got it upstairs."

After a long and very hard stare, Mel put on a shaky smile. "Oh... yeah." Whatever silent communication had just happened between the two of them, Justin had a feeling Mel would be giving her daughter a butterfly necklace.

Charlie slipped through the doorway and sidled up to Justin just as Natalie launched herself into Mel's embrace.

"I'm so glad you came," whispered Mel.

"I told you to give me five minutes," Justin murmured in Charlie's ear.

"Old man, I gave you seven and a half minutes," she hissed back. "That girl wasn't gonna stay put a second longer."

"What's going on?" asked Sandy, coming up behind them.

The narrow hallway was getting mighty congested. "Is there a reason we're holding this gathering in the hallway?" asked Justin, frowning.

With a bit of laughter and some starts and stops, the group flowed back toward the sitting room. Justin stopped at the hallway closet and pulled out his daddy's guitar, and then he followed the rest of the group.

"I think that's enough reading for one day," he announced as he stepped into the room and held the guitar over his head.

"Wait!" Sandy held up a hand. "What did Greta and Keagan name their baby?"

Justin snorted. "I can answer that. Wolfe Neil McGee. My granddaddy. Now let's get this sing-along in gear!"

Ryan and Sean were already moving the coffee table to one side while Sandy and Mel pulled pillows and cushions off the love seat and chairs.

"What are they doing?" asked Natalie, her gaze flitting around the room like a nervous hummingbird.

"Do you like to sing?" asked Charlie, drawing the teen with her to an overstuffed green tweed cushion off to the side.

"Not... um, not too much." She leaned toward Charlie and lowered her voice. "I'm not very good."

Charlie's explosive chortle seemed to bounce off the walls. "Neither am I, hon." She dropped to the floor and leaned against the cushion then patted the rug with her palm. "So you just park yourself here next to me, and no one'll know which of us is singin' off key."

Chapter Nine

"Twelve drummers drumming," belted out Charlie with the rest of the group. "Eleven pipers..."

"...lords a-leap—" sang Sean in his rich baritone.

Mel smacked his shoulder "Pipers!"

A baffled expression crossed his face. "It is?"

"Nine ladies dancing," Sandy made a point of singing in Sean's face.

"Wait!" Ryan held up a hand. "I thought it was nine maids a-milking and eight ladies dancing."

The singing stopped, but Justin kept the guitar going. Was he hopeful the argument would get worked out any quicker on this run-through than it had on the previous three? Or was he just insane?

"The ladies were next to the lords," offered Nattie helpfully.

"Oh! Right, the ones that were piping." Sean struck his temple with the heel of his hand.

"The pipers were piping, you idiot!" Mel tapped Sean's other temple.

"Ten of them?" he asked, raising his eyebrows and darting a hopeful glance at Sandy.

"Eleven!" shouted the group in unison as Ryan pitched a green grape from the snack tray at his brother. It bounced off the top of Sean's head and left him blinking.

Sandy batted Ryan's fingers away when he reached for another grape. "Really? After you just wasted the last one?"

"Five *gold*...en ri-i-ings!" Ricky blasted over the fray.

Charlie gave an approving nod. Good for him. Everyone knew what came next after the rings. She hoped.

"Four calling birds," sang everyone pleasantly.

"Three turtle—oomph." Sean glared at his wife.

Finally, they hit the last line. "And a partridge in a pear tree."

Justin played a few complicated chords and then leaned the guitar against the side of his chair.

"Whew!" Sandy collapsed backward onto a pile of pillows. "I thought we'd never make it."

"We almost didn't," noted Ryan, handing Bethany a juice box.

"This reminds me of a Christmas pageant I was in when I was a kid," said Sandy, springing back to an upright position.

"Tell us!" squeaked out Mel. She turned to Natalie. "You *have* to hear Sandy tell a story."

"Well, let's see... it happened back in Virginia when I was ten — no, eleven! The weather was exceptionally warm for December, even in the South, and my mom's garden still had a few flowers hanging on. But even though it didn't *seem* like Christmas was just around the corner, I knew it was."

A smile tugged at Charlie's lips. The woman was as good at telling stories as she was at singing. Charlie settled back into her seat, ready to enjoy the tale.

Bethany crawled into Sandy's lap, and she shifted the little girl before continuing in a dreamy voice. "It was the first year I got a solo singing part in the Christmas program at church. *Hark! The Herald Angels Sing*. I practiced for weeks just to get the part."

Her eyes took on a faraway shine, and she sighed. "It was going to be the best pageant ever. Pastor Ainsley had this great idea to use real animals. Not farm animals, but pets dressed up like them. I hounded my mom for days, begging her to let us use our dogs, Sugar and Spice. They were standard poodles. You know, the big kind? They were pure white, and when they hadn't been groomed, they looked a little like sheep."

She grimaced and rolled her eyes. "At least I thought so when I squinted at them really hard. Anyway, Mama finally gave in but she made me promise to brush them out and give them baths." She grinned. "Of course, being eleven, I promptly forgot all of her instructions until the last minute. So there we were on the day of the pageant, brushing knots from their coats and pulling out burs."

A chuckle burst from Mel. "That must be why you're such a stickler for getting everything done early now."

"Ha!" Ryan picked up Sandy's hand and kissed her wrist. "A lot you know. She hasn't even stuffed the turkey yet."

"Oh, goodness! You're right. Maybe I should get up right now and go make the stuffing." Sandy shifted and moved to settle Bethany on Ryan's lap, but he stopped her.

"Never mind... you might as well finish the story." He deflected Bethany back to Sandy by standing and crossing to the fireplace.

Sandy smiled and sent Justin a wink. His mouth curved upward on one side.

Oh yeah, she had the McGee family right where she wanted them.

"So we took Sugar and Spice to the rehearsals, and since they were show dogs, they were very well behaved. Spice was always more friendly than his sister, but even Sugar made friends with the music director." Sandy picked up her mug of cocoa and took a sip. "Then Scott Upton convinced his uncle to let us borrow *his* dog so we could dress her up like the donkey. He just showed up with her the day of the pageant..."

* * *

The creature stood in the middle of the Sunday School room where the pageant cast had gathered. It had four legs and something that might pass for fur covering its massive body, and it let out a throaty "woof" when Sugar and Spice approached, which seemed to indicate it belonged to the canine family.

"What kind of dog *is* that?" asked Sandy, wrinkling her nose and eyeing the shaggy monster. Coarse gray fur covered its entire body from the tip of its swishing tail to the scruffy beard on its nose.

"She's an Irish wolfhound," answered the boy with a grin on his face. "Won't she make a great donkey?"

Well... the beast was big enough to *ride* like a donkey. "What's her name?"

"Izzy." Scott tugged the brown robe over his head and transformed into Joseph.

"Hello, Izzy." Sandy held out her hand, palm-up.

A low growl issued from Sugar's throat, so Sandy dropped her hand and gave the leash a gentle tug. "Shhh. Sit."

With a whine of protest, the poodle sat.

Izzy slowly turned her head and regarded Sandy with deep brown eyes. Then she gazed at Sugar, opened her mouth for a long yawn that ended with a tiny squeak, and also sat.

Clapping her hands, Mrs. Brentwood, the pageant director, entered the room and called for everyone's attention. Fluorescent overhead lights made her gray hair look a little bluer than usual. "Okay, I need everyone to line up the way we practiced."

With shuffling feet and rustling cloth, they all moved through the double doors at the rear of the sanctuary and stepped onto the pale blue carpeting that almost matched Mrs. Brentwood's hair.

John Small and Monique Rogers, two of the eighth graders, stepped in front of the microphone at the pulpit.

In a quivery voice, Monique began to read. "'And it came to pass in those days, that there went out a decree from Caesar Augustus that all the world should be taxed.'"

John was a bit less shaky as he took over in a deep voice that occasionally squeaked. "'And all went to be taxed, every one into his own city. And Joseph also went up from Galilee, out of the city of Nazareth, into Judaea, unto the city of David, which is called Bethlehem; to be taxed with Mary his espoused wife, being great with child."'

Organ music began and the congregation was directed to stand. As they sang *O' Come Emmanuel*, Scott Upton led Izzy up the center aisle of the sanctuary while Cindy Hart trudged beside him.

A few people pointed and smiled at the pair as they plodded up the aisle, and some of the smaller children reached out toward Izzy. From the front of the sanctuary, off to the left, Mrs. Brentwood frantically motioned until Scott draped an arm over Cindy's shoulders so it appeared "Joseph" was helping "Mary" along.

And Cindy certainly needed help, because gravity was staking a claim to the padding she wore beneath her blue cotton robe.

Sandy's eyes widened as little by little the bulge slipped downward. Bending over, Cindy clutched the padding and gave a mighty shove upward. She managed to keep it in place by dragging her right foot, creating a hunched-over limp that resembled that of Dr. Frankenstein's assistant.

Mrs. Brentwood covered her eyes and peeked through her fingers.

Finally the couple made it to the front of the sanctuary, and not a moment too soon. The congregation finished singing, and "Mary" was delivered of a green-and-gold striped pillow, which dropped to the floor at Cindy's feet. She gave a sheepish smile as Scott kicked the pillow off to the side. Then Scott assisted Cindy to sit behind the wooden manger. Izzy promptly sat, too, suddenly looking far less like a donkey.

Monique took up the narration again. "'And so it was, that, while they were there, the days were accomplished that she should be delivered. And she brought forth her firstborn son, and wrapped him in swaddling clothes, and laid him in a manger; because there was no room for them in the inn.'"

Cindy pulled a doll from under the manger and flipped it into the straw, then leaned on the wooden crib and heaved a dramatic sigh. The tinkling strains of the piano began, and the children's choir, dressed up as a host of angels, marched through the door from Pastor Ainsley's office behind the pulpit singing *Away in a Manger.*

That was the cue for Sandy and her two fellow shepherds, Mason North and Faith Hayes, to move up the right side aisle so they could get into position in the "shepherd's field" in front of the pipe organ As Sandy started forward, the bottom of her plastic shepherd's hook jammed against the base of a pew and poked her in the stomach, sending the air whooshing from her lungs.

Tears welled, but she stemmed them as she gasped for breath, stumbling for a couple of steps. Sugar angled her head upward and regarded Sandy with concern in her chocolate colored eyes. Then she licked Sandy's hand as if to offer moral support, and they managed to regain their rhythm. Still a little breathless by the time they made it to the front, Sandy positioned herself on the tiny piece of tape that had been stuck to the carpeting so she would know where to stand.

"'And there were in the same country shepherds abiding in the field, keeping watch over their flock by night,'" read John.

Mason shielded his eyes and peered around the congregation like a hunter on safari, while Faith and Sandy pretended to talk to each other. Sugar sat and scratched.

Monique picked up the narrative. "'And, lo, the angel of the Lord came upon them, and the glory of the Lord shone round about them: and they were sore afraid.'"

Sandy affected a soft gasp. Faith cringed and held her hands in front of her face, looking like she was ducking a slap to the head, while Mason clutched his cheeks, his mouth forming a giant O.

Dressed all in white and sprinkled with silver and gold glitter, Faith's little sister Gracie sat in the first pew, kicking her feet back and forth and making faces at Sugar. Her angel wings were bent, and the band holding her halo rested askew on her head, causing the gold wire circle to dangle over her right ear.

The sanctuary fell into an expectant silence.

Gracie only had two lines. All she had to do was stand up and say her first one, and that would lead into Sandy's solo. Gracie wrinkled her nose and stuck her tongue out at the dog.

Monique cleared her throat and added a little bite to her voice. "'And they were sore afraid.'"

Again silence fell.

Sandy nudged Faith and nodded at Gracie. "Do something," she mouthed.

"Gracie," whispered Faith.

"'They were *sore afraid*,'" repeated Monique loudly.

"Grace!" hissed Faith, using her shepherd's hook to poke her sister's foot. "Say your line!"

Big blue eyes grew even wider as Gracie scrambled to stand up on the pew. "Don't be scairt!" she screeched like a witch. "I have goo-oo-ood news. Mary had a baby!"

Sandy's jaw dropped at the flubbed lines. Gracie had played her role perfectly in all the rehearsals. What had happened? Faith nudged Sandy with her elbow and whispered, "Sing."

Soft piano was already playing the opening chords of her solo! Oh, no! How did the song start? She squeezed her eyes closed and tried to call the words to mind, but the brightly dancing notes overpowered her memory.

The music stopped abruptly.

"Oh, my," someone in the congregation whispered.

Sugar scratched again and then snapped loudly at her right hindquarter.

"Bless her heart," another person murmured, sending Sandy an encouraging smile. "She has stage fright."

I do not! She pressed her lips together to keep from yelling the denial out loud.

Mrs. Brentwood gave an encouraging nod. Bold chords rang through the sanctuary again, and Sandy drew a breath, ready to sing. What was that word...?

Her memory lit up like a bolt of lightning. "Hark!" Sandy shouted. Heat flooded into her cheeks. "Um... I mean..." She closed her eyes and listened to the piano, allowed the melody and rhythm to fill her. And then she began to sing. "Hark! The herald angels sing, glory to the newborn king..."

The words flowed through her as she sang the carol. She performed even better than she had in practice. Sandy's heart swelled with pride. The congregation seemed to sigh with her as the last note faded.

This time Gracie was ready. "Go see Mary's baby. He's right over there." She swept her arm in a dramatic arc and pointed at the manger. Her halo tumbled to the floor. "Oh, damn it!" She jumped from the pew amid the collective gasps of the congregation.

Sandy stole a peek at Mrs. Brentwood in time to catch the pageant director burying her face in one palm.

"Let us go forth and visit the babe," said Mason in a voice loud enough to be heard from the street.

Sandy and Faith nodded, and as they began an exaggeratedly slow march toward the manger, Mr. Dyson, a music teacher at the high school, began to strum his guitar. Three eighth graders walked up the center aisle dressed as wise men in rich velour robes. Their voices were strong and sure as they sang, "We three kings of Orient are bearing gifts, we traverse afar..."

Sandy and the other shepherds arrived at the manger. While they waited for the kings to arrive, they pointed at the baby and sighed. Spice stretched his nose toward Izzy and began wagging his plumed tail.

With her solo behind her, Sandy's mind began to drift. As the wise men joined them at the manger and gave their gifts, she mentally traced the pictures in the stained glass window. Her arm developed a tickle and she scratched it away.

"We shall tell the world about the babe we found in the manger," said one of the wise men.

"'Mary kept all these things, and pondered them in her heart,'" Monique finished with a gusty sigh.

John leaned in to the microphone. "Please stand and join us in singing *Joy to the World*."

Rustles and shuffles and whispers raced through the sanctuary as the congregation rose. The organist played a little trumpet flare, and the singing began.

Sandy's itch returned, a little higher up, and she rubbed at the spot. Next to her, Sugar sat and scratched her neck and then nearly doubled over and began chewing one hind leg. Over the sounds of the music rose sucking, slurping sounds.

"Stop that," whispered Sandy, jiggling the leash, but the chewing continued.

Spice stood and sniffed the air. A soft whine issued from his throat.

Sugar stopped her chewing and stared at Sandy.

As the third verse began, Spice started pulling. What was he so interested in? Glancing over her shoulder, Sandy didn't notice anything unusual. Izzy sat next to Scott, ears pricked forward. Why was Spice so interested in the giant gray beast?

"Scott," whispered Sandy.

Apparently not hearing her, he kept singing.

Clenching her teeth, Sandy reined Spice in and wrapped the leash one more time around her hand, just in case. An itch began in the center of her back, and she wiggled her shoulder blades, but it didn't go away

Sugar scratched at her neck with renewed determination then flopped to her side and rolled onto her back, squirming and wiggling, legs shooting straight up in the air. She looked like a break dancing rag mop.

"Stop that," ordered Sandy through gritted teeth. The dog's itching was making her itch more. Something tiny and dark scuttled across the dog's belly. Sandy leaned closer. The dark speck joined another dark speck and both burrowed into the curly fur. Oh, no. No, it couldn't be.

Fleas!

The itch on Sandy's back intensified as she imagined herself crawling with hundreds of the disgusting insects.

The congregation stopped singing and sat, and Paster Ainsley stepped up to the pulpit. "Do we have any prayer requests?"

Sandy had one, but perhaps it wasn't the time to pray for the fleas to go away.

The pastor swiped one hand across the back of his neck and then stepped down and strolled along the center aisle, calling on people and listening to their concerns. As he leaned over, listening to an elderly woman with blue hair, he absently scratched his upper arm.

Dread tightened Sandy's throat until she couldn't swallow. She struggled just to breathe as she remembered him petting Sugar and Spice and giving Sugar a brisk belly rub when they'd arrived that morning.

The itch on her back shifted to a spot behind her ear. She nudged the area with her shoulder.

I am not covered in fleas. I am not covered in fleas. I am not covered in fleas.

A tickle began in her armpit. No *way* would she scratch *there*. She squeezed her arm against her body and moved it back and forth.

"What are you doing?" asked Faith softly.

Before Sandy could answer, Pastor Ainsley returned to the pulpit. "Let us pray."

More shuffling emanated from the congregation as parishioners bowed their heads and waited. But Sandy's eyes were on Pastor, squinting, searching for any sign of moving dark specks.

Spice inched toward Izzy again. Pressing her lips together, Sandy checked her grip on his leash.

Faith nudged her. "What are you doing?" she asked again.

"Sugar has fleas," whispered Sandy.

"What did you say?"

Sandy tried again. "The dogs have fleas."

"What are you saying?" Faith stepped close. "I can't hear you."

"Amen." Pastor Ainsley finished the prayer.

"Amen," echoed the people.

"I said... *we have fleas!*" The words echoed throughout the hushed sanctuary. Horror engulfed Sandy as murmurs rose.

Pastor Ainsley stopped in mid-scratch of his lower arm and stared at Sandy, slack-jawed. Finally, he managed a weak, "Oh, dear."

Almost as one, the parishioners began squirming and scratching. Warmth swamped Sandy's face. Her mom was going to kill her. If not because she'd forgotten to bathe Sugar and Spice, then surely for interrupting the church service.

Do something!

Sandy stepped to the microphone John and Monique had used. She didn't wait for the people to quiet down. Too many were jumping around, crying out about itching and how it was a bad idea to bring animals into a church. It was pure chaos and she had caused it.

Drawing in a deep breath, she began to sing her favorite Christmas song. "What child is this, who laid to rest...?"

Ms. Martha started playing a quiet accompaniment on the organ. By the time they reached the second verse, everyone had settled back into their seats. A few even smiled at her. An itch started in the small of her back but she tried not to think about it.

At the end of the song, the congregation sat in silence for a minute and then burst into thunderous applause. Sandy's heart swelled. Maybe she'd managed to save the day after all.

Someone tugged on the sleeve of her robe. "Sandy..." Gracie stared up at her, blue eyes wide as saucers.

"Just a minute, Gracie." Sandy wanted to revel in the adoration just a moment longer.

"But Sandy..." The little girl tugged again. She was going to ruin the moment, since she would likely keep pestering until Sandy gave her some attention.

"What?"

"Why is the sheep-doggie stuck to the donkey-doggie?" asked Gracie, full-volume.

Mrs. Brentwood slumped to the floor with a dull thud.

* * *

Justin covered a yawn with a soft chuckle as Sandy finished her story. The fire was making him drowsy. The story, however, had brought on his own fond memories of a misspent childhood.

"Of course, there was no way we could have infested the whole congregation, but since no one really knew for sure, everyone rushed out of there without any fellowship after the service." Sandy grinned. "We weren't exactly unwelcome in church after that, but wherever we sat, we had the pew to ourselves."

Mel's eyes glittered with mischief. "And by the sheep-doggie stuck to the donkey-doggie, you mean...?"

"Oh, yes, nine weeks later, Izzy had seven puppies. Scraggly, gray, curly fur, droopy ears, and *huge* feet." A sigh slipped out. "Scott and I worked really hard finding them homes. Not many people want a dog that's going to be eighty pounds of sass and bad fur. And after that, we were never allowed to see each other again." Her grin returned. "Of course, that rule only guaranteed that we ended up going to senior prom together."

"Is this past love someone I should be concerned about?" Ryan asked with a lazy chuckle.

"Only if you feel threatened by carpet salesmen," sang out Sandy. "He owns three carpet stores in Virginia. Calls himself the Blue Ridge Carpet King."

With a loud pop, a log split in the fireplace, sending a shower of sparks up the chimney.

Bethany had nodded off and lay with her face buried in her mama's shoulder. Sandy brushed a few dark curls off the sleeping toddler's face and smiled. In a soft voice, she began singing, "What child is this...?"

Justin picked up his guitar and strummed a soft accompaniment as he swept his gaze around the room. Faces watched his daughter-in-law with rapt admiration. Mel sat in Sean's arms, rocking Mitchell. Suddenly Natalie scooted over to join them, laying her blond head on her mother's shoulder with a sigh.

When he shifted his glance to the right a bit, he caught Charlie regarding him with a soft look in her eyes. His lips pulled up on one side as he nodded acknowledgement. Crimson invaded her cheeks, and she quickly looked away. His half-smile became a full-fledged grin.

Chapter Ten

"Just heard the weather forecast on the radio," announced Sandy, striding back into the living room after a brief break in the kitchen. "They've closed the interstates, including I-80."

Justin brought his head up sharply. "That far south?"

"Apparently." Sandy smiled at Ryan. "Good thing you guys got in when you did, or you might have missed Christmas." She stepped up to the window and pulled back the curtain.

The glimpse Justin caught brought on a shiver. Dusk had fallen, but the blanket of white made it look more like mid-afternoon. Gusts of wind had sent drifts all the way onto the front porch, even under the awning. He turned away from the icy scene and studied the eight-foot tree they'd decorated a couple of weeks back. Covered from top to base in shiny glass ornaments that had been in his family for years, the tree also had some extra touches Sandy had shared from her own family. Lights of all colors and tiny blinking white lights put out enough room to read a book by. And along with the rope of golden garland, Sandy had added red plaid ribbons edged in gold spiraling down from the top of the tree. Instead of the cherubic angel on a gossamer cloud that he'd been accustomed to for more than half a century, a white teddy bear with shiny silver wings clung to the top. He'd never seen any tree decorated quite like theirs, but it sure was pretty.

Proof that things could change but still be as nice.

"What about you, Ryan?" asked Natalie as the conversation drifted toward silence. She leaned forward eagerly. "Do you have a special Christmas memory?"

"Every Christmas was the best," said Ryan. Firelight flickered over his face, and green eyes — so very like his mom's — sparkled as he paused, perhaps gathering his thoughts. "Mom and Dad always made it special." He shot Justin a grin. "Always something different, yet the same. We never knew exactly what to expect, but we knew it would be perfect. Even after—" His voice caught.

Justin fought back tears. Beth had been the light of his life. Her untimely death had robbed him of that, and also robbed their sons of the best mother they could have asked for. Suddenly, Mel's insecurity made sense. For in the back of his mind, he'd always thought he'd failed Beth by not keeping her safe.

Sandy shifted Bethany and snuggled against his shoulder with a soft sigh, but her sympathetic eyes remained fixed on Justin, and she smiled.

In a natural move, Ryan pressed a kiss to the top of his wife's head. Then he squared his shoulders and looked up, also meeting Justin's gaze. "After it was just Dad, he made sure Christmas was magical."

Pride overflowed in Justin's heart, not in himself for holding the traditions of Christmas together, but in his son for overlooking all the times he'd fallen short.

"So which Christmas stands out the most for you?" asked Mel as she handed Mitchell a musical choo-choo.

Mitchell pushed one of the train's buttons and was rewarded by a thin whistle. He chortled and pushed it again. But suddenly he dropped it in favor of the — thankfully quieter — push car.

A haunted look shadowed Ryan's eyes and twisted his mouth. Justin almost wished for the relief of the toddler's noisy toy.

When Ryan spoke, his voice was low, intensified by emotion. "That first Christmas after I left home... I wasn't sure I'd ever see Sean or Dad again. I knew I wouldn't see them for a long time, anyway."

Sean settled a hand on Ryan's shoulder. From her place on the floor next to him, Mel snuck her hand into Justin's and squeezed. A lump of emotion built in his throat.

"We were in Texas, in a little town outside Abilene. Clyde." Ryan stared into the fire. "We were out of money so we didn't have a choice but to stop. I could only hope we'd gotten far enough." He heaved a sigh. Speaking was obviously growing difficult, but he plowed on. "For a little while, at least. I got a job as a cook in a Huddle Hut. Told everyone Mac was my little brother and our parents had died." Slowly he shook his head. "I don't think I was fooling the manager, Kari Belton. But she didn't ask questions. She hired Mac to bus tables and wash dishes, and paid us under the table. And she let us stay in her garage."

"A garage?" Charlie tilted her head sideways and frowned. "Like a converted apartment?"

Ryan barked out a laugh that echoed off the ceiling. Charlie jumped and clutched for the arm of the sofa.

"The place was a freakin' dump," said Ryan, still laughing, though he toned it down a bit. "She had to move her car and lay cardboard on the oil puddle to give us a place to sleep." Then the laughter ended in a gentle sigh, and he shook his head. "But her husband had worked on cars in there, and he'd had a bathroom put in so he could clean up before going in the house. She gave us a space heater, and we had sleeping bags." He shrugged as if it didn't matter. "We made it work."

Using the thumb of his free hand, Justin wiped at his eyes. With movements he barely noticed at first, Charlie moved until she and Mel flanked him. Then she took up his other hand and laced their fingers together.

The warmth of her touch eased the dull ache that was growing in his heart. He didn't pull away as Ryan continued the story.

"Little by little, Miss Kari and her husband Dale gave us things. We'd just come home and find them. I almost cried when we found a pair of twin beds with saggy old mattresses." A smile played at the corners of his mouth, and his shoulders relaxed. "That was the week before Christmas. I tried not to show Mac how homesick I was feeling. Tried to make it an adventure. But he knew. It didn't seem like Christmas was any big deal for him. I guess, considering where he came from..." His lips twisted into a wry smile. "So I pretended it wasn't a big deal for me either. Huddle Hut was open Christmas Day — the only restaurant in town that was. And it was hopping for such a small town. So we worked. But that was okay because on work days, our meals were free."

* * *

Most of the rush had passed and the night shift staff arrived by the time Ryan and Mac got their Christmas dinner. Perry Como serenaded restaurant-goers about being home during the holidays, while Ryan stared at the T-bone on his plate. He couldn't recall ever having anything but turkey on Christmas Day. But food was food, and he was hungry, so with a shrug, he sawed into the tender broiled meat. *First time for everything.*

After all, he'd never been away from his dad and Sean on the holiday either.

Without a word — or apparently any second thoughts — Mac scarfed down his shrimp and fries basket. When they got home, Ryan would give him the gift he'd picked up at the gas station. It wasn't much; he hadn't been able to spare more than a couple of dollars, but Mac was really just a kid. He should have something for Christmas.

"Th-th-this is g-good." The sixteen-year-old set his fork down with a metallic clatter and grabbed his chocolate shake.

"Yeah, better than Ramen on the hot plate."

"I-I'm s-sorry, R-Ryan. Y-you prob-probably m-miss h-home." He was worked up. He always stuttered more when he thought too much or let things get to him.

"Slow down." Ryan grinned. "This is home for now, and we're here so it's kinda hard to miss it." He popped the last bite of steak into his mouth and chewed. After he finished off his soda, he stood and stacked their plates. "I'll help you wash these up so we can head on home."

It was only two blocks to home — a.k.a. Kari's garage — and they accomplished the walk quickly. As Mac turned on their only lamp, Ryan flipped the switch on the heater to stave off the coming evening chill.

A cry of surprise rose from the other side of the garage, and Ryan whirled around. Mac stood in front of a long beige couch that hadn't been there when they'd left for the day. Worn patches in the arms and a long jagged tear across the top didn't detract from the welcome gift.

Then Mac stepped aside, revealing a twelve-inch black-and-white TV sitting on a low table across from the sofa. A piece of paper was taped to the front. Ryan could read the dark block letters from across the room.

It works. Enjoy. Merry Christmas. ~K and D

Mac's gaze flicked between the sofa and the TV as if he didn't know which to check out first. Finally, he pushed the television's ON button and waited while the snow adjusted itself into shadowy black-and-white images moving across the screen.

Ryan glanced at the blue plastic grocery bag he'd stashed next to the hot plate on the work bench. He'd managed to scrape together a few dollars to get Mac a present, but he'd never found the moment to give it to him. The bag was cool against his palm.

Canned laughter burst from the TV, and Mac chuckled along with it, a real chuckle, not the ones he usually forced. Maybe the time for gifts had passed. They'd had their family moment back at Huddle Hut.

The bag went back to its unassuming place on the makeshift kitchen counter in favor of the bag of chips and the half-eaten tub of dip — payday splurges — from the mini-fridge beneath the bench. Ryan sauntered over to the sofa and lowered himself down on one end then set the chips and dip on the center cushion.

After checking out all the channels, Mac discovered they had two that came in clearly with only minor adjustment to the rabbit ears, and a third that came in accompanied by a lot of static no matter what they did.

Mac chose one of the clearer ones and flopped on the other end of the couch. To the crunching of chips, a family sitcom played out on the tiny TV screen. During a commercial with Santa Claus riding an electric razor over snowy hills, Mac rose and walked to his bed. Maybe the kid was tired. Come to think of it, Ryan was ready to hit the pillow himself.

But Mac returned in just a couple of minutes, holding a small oblong box wrapped in red and white paper and topped by a small gold bow. "This is for you," he said, holding out the gift.

Ryan bolted up from his slouch. "What did you do, kid?"

Crimson splashed across Mac's freckled cheeks. "It-it's n-not m-much, but..." He shrugged and pushed the present into Ryan's hands. "And th-they were even h-half off at the M-marathon station."

Warmth stole over Ryan as he loosened the tape from one end and slid out a tan faux leather case. When he flipped open the lid, a pair of aviator sunglasses stared up at him. They didn't look all that cheap, half off or not. With trembling hands, he reached in and plucked them from their blue velveteen resting place.

"I... don't know what to say." He lifted his gaze to his cousin. "Thank you."

"Y-you s-squint a l-lot. Wh-when y-you're out in the s-sun," explained Mac with a one-shoulder shrug.

And the bright sun sometimes gave him headaches, too, but Ryan hadn't realized Mac had noticed. Grinning, he shoved the glasses on. "How do I look?"

Mac chuckled. "B-bad ass, man. L-like Iceman from *Top Gun.*"

As comparisons went, Ryan supposed he could do worse than Val Kilmer.

"I, um..." He slipped the glasses off and replaced them in the case, then pushed to his feet. "I got something for you, too." He forestalled Mac's protests with one hand and a shake of his head as he walked to their crude kitchenette. The plastic bag looked pathetic in comparison to the care Mac had taken with his gift. "I didn't have a chance to wrap it."

Plastic rustled as Mac grasped the bag and opened it. With a delighted exclamation, he withdrew a thick book bound in red cloth and a package of cheap ballpoint pens.

"It's blank inside," Ryan explained, shifting from foot-to-foot. "I saw that you like to write stuff and you save scratch paper from work."

Dim lamplight gleamed off Mac's blue eyes as a brilliant smile burst across his face. "Th-thanks!" He stepped close, and they shared a hug but just a brief one.

Ryan patted his cousin on the back as they drew apart. "We shoulda got a Christmas tree."

"Yeah..." Mac grinned. "N-next year, right?"

"Next year," agreed Ryan as they walked back to the sofa.

* * *

From the corner of her eye, Charlie watched Justin as Ryan fell into silence. He seemed to be holding up okay, though that couldn't have been an easy story to listen to. She glanced away quickly so he wouldn't catch her staring at him again. It wouldn't do for him to know she looked at him often these days. After his heart attack, they'd spent more time together. There'd even been a couple of "moments." At least Charlie had thought they'd had some moments where they'd seemed on the precipice of something... more.

She was ready for more, would welcome it. They'd both been widowed for years. Being alone for the rest of her life was an uncomfortable proposition. She and Justin had lots in common, and there must be *some* reason her heart thumped a little harder and faster whenever he was near.

But in the past couple of months, Justin had kind of backed off from their friendship. It had happened after a trip to Jackson with Ryan, almost as though he'd left that day and come back different. The same person... only changed. Distant. Where had her best friend gone?

"You still have those glasses," murmured Sandy, drawing Charlie from her musings. It hadn't been a question.

"I do," agreed Ryan with a sad smile.

Charlie's heart stalled. It was probably one of the few pieces of his cousin that Ryan had left. Mac had died in the aftermath of an earthquake, working alongside Ryan as a firefighter in California.

"Did you get a tree the next year?" blurted Ricky, scooting to the edge of his seat in one of the leather armchairs framing the fireplace.

Ryan tossed him a grin. "Yep! The next year and every year after until..." He shrugged.

"What did he used to write?" pressed the teenager.

"Short stories, letters he never sent. Thoughts." Ryan shrugged. "Poetry."

The sadness lifted some with several exclamations of surprise.

"I read what he'd let me," said Ryan, shifting his arm to settle it more tightly around Sandy. "Some he kept private. But what I read... he was a gifted writer." He focused his gaze on Ricky. "He wrote mostly about your mom."

The remains of Charlie's heart fractured. For years, everyone in Orson's Folly had labored under the falsehood that Mac had run off and left his girlfriend at the time — Ricky's mother — pregnant and alone. Mac's older brother had stepped up, or rather been pushed by the family, and Brenda had suffered marriage to a drunken brute. But the real secret, the one no one had seen coming, was that Mac wasn't Ricky's father, but his brother, and Ricky was really the product of rape by the abusive MacKay patriarch.

Ugh! The mood was quickly fading into maudlin. *Do something, Charlie!*

"Did anyone see the light display at City Hall?" she pretty much shouted.

"Light display?" asked Mel. "You mean the string of colored lights over the door?"

"Oh, no..." Charlie warmed up to the tale. "Cedar garland, rope lights along the fence, and twinklers in the bushes. Probably a thousand lights out there now."

"Two thousand." Justin covered the statement with a cough.

"Mayor Kelly said he doesn't know who did—" Charlie's breath caught. "You, old man? *You* put lights on City Hall?"

Justin pushed his arms over his head and stretched. "Look at the time. Think we might get some dinner soon?"

"Lasagna should be done." Sandy's voice about dripped with relief. "Who wants to help set the table?" She pinned Ricky and Nattie in her gaze and smiled. That hadn't really been a question either.

Chapter Eleven

Soft jazzy Christmas music played in the background as everyone took a seat at the kitchen table. After the shuffling and scraping of chairs died down, new sounds began. Silverware clinked against china as plates were loaded and platters passed. Justin stole a sideways glance at Sandy. Would she stop him from taking an extra helping of lasagna?

She caught his eye. "I made spinach lasagna with low-fat cheese."

Sean suppressed a groan.

A slow smile warmed Sandy's face. "But then I decided to eat healthy next week, so I froze that one and went for a more traditional recipe. So eat as much as y'all want..." She winked at Justin. "But don't step on the scales for a couple of days."

Justin grinned as the warmth of family love spread through him. Winking back at his daughter-in-law, he took her at her word and heaped his plate with layers of pasta, sauce, and cheese, and then plucked not one, but two of her homemade rolls from the basket. And he'd slather real butter on those rolls, too, by golly, lots of it.

Gentle laughter and the rise and fall of murmured conversation and random teasing set the mood as Justin finished filling his plate.

The kitchen in the old ranch house had always been a natural gathering place. Didn't matter if the occasion was happy, sad, or in between. It seemed like they always gravitated there. The old oak table had been in the family since long before he'd been born, built by his grandfather at the old homestead. It got a facelift every generation or so, but no one had seemed eager to replace it.

As his family gathered around that table now, a sense of satisfaction filled Justin. Life didn't get much better than seeing it continue in children and grandchildren.

"What about you, Dad?" asked Ricky, stirring Justin from his musing. "What Christmas do you remember most?"

A chuckle slipped out. "Boy, when you get to be my age, they either all blend into one big holiday, or your mind starts making stuff up."

"Bah!" Seated next to him, Charlie poked him in the shoulder. "Don't give me that. Your mind is sharper than a wood tack and just as prickly."

Tingles raced along his arm from the point of contact, and Justin masked his shiver of awareness by sprinkling some grated Romano cheese over his lasagna. He set the canister back on the table and paused. His hand ached to reach over and take hold of Charlie's, just to see how she'd react.

Or how anyone would react, for that matter. He slid his gaze to Ryan and then Sean, both engaged in conversations with their respective children.

And he chickened out. Again.

Better to take the safe road. So instead of taking Charlie by the hand, he reached for a fresh-baked roll, making the total count three of them lining the edge of his plate. "I do have fond memories of one particularly eventful Christmas when I was a boy... back in fifth grade."

Charlie's gasp told Justin he'd struck gold on the memoir scale.

"What happened in the fifth grade, Dad?" asked Ricky, gesturing with his fork before spearing a bite of lasagna.

"I kinda want to know that myself." Sean eyed him with a speculative gaze. "Being as you've mentioned something about the fifth grade before but never explained."

A snort came from Ryan's direction. "Knowing Dad, the real story started years before Christmas. It could take a while to tell."

"Ayup... it might. But it only started about a month before Christmas." He shoveled some green beans into his mouth and chewed. Slowly. After he swallowed, he took a forkful of lasagna and followed that with a sip of the Chianti that Sandy had served up. Not bad, he thought, nodding. He usually preferred iced tea with his meal, but the wine really did seem to enhance the taste of the food.

"Told you," murmured Ryan, and he lifted his own glass of wine to his lips.

"Shhh, maybe he's trying to remember," offered Sean in a stage whisper.

That earned him a glare from Mel as she snagged the roll from his plate and handed it to Mitchell.

"Hey!" cried Sean, but it was too late. His son took a giant bite and then grinned around pieces of bread.

"Oh, I recall just fine." Justin nudged Charlie. "I'll bet so does Ms. Charlie. We were both ten and only a year or so before I was still thinking of girls as having cooties. They weren't supposed to be competitive, and I had no idea they could hold onto grudges."

"*I* was competitive?" squeaked Charlie. "I deserved to win that science fair, and you know it!" She shot him an outraged glare. "I would have, too, if my box of baking soda hadn't disappeared."

"Hey, one box of baking soda looks just like another." Justin shrugged. "How was I to know the difference? And my volcano was just as good as yours. Plus I had dinosaurs in my diorama." He chomped down hard on a roll and enjoyed her glaring at him as he chewed.

"Children, children, fight nicely," offered Ryan in a mild tone. "Remember to use your words."

Justin shot his former nemesis a grin. "Started about the middle of November, didn't it?"

"I'd just moved to Orson's Folly with my parents," said Charlie, sopping up some sauce with her roll. "And I wanted to make a really grand impression."

"Oh, you made an impression..." said Justin, keeping his voice bland.

* * *

As soon as Justin saw the other volcano, his heart sank. He'd been so certain he'd be the only one in the science fair to make one. He squared his shoulders and marched across the gym to the far end of the table, away from the other display, and set his down. He'd get set up and then go look into the competition.

With great care, he laid out his diorama, adjusting the plastic trees and bushes he'd made by tearing apart a fake flower arrangement his mother had gotten from the dime store. It looked pretty cool. Too bad the only dinosaurs he'd found were weird colors. But he shrugged as he adjusted a family of triceratops around a giant nest made of pieces of straw. Because who knew, really, that some dinosaurs hadn't had blue skin?

He dug his box of baking soda out of the shopping bag, opened it, and dumped it into the empty bean can hidden in the center of his volcano. Then he played with the vegetation a little more until it hid the rim of the can.

"That's a pretty neat setup," said a soft voice from behind him.

Startled, Justin whirled about and came face-to-face with a girl about his own age. Blue eyes gleamed as she regarded him, taking his measure. Dark brown hair spilled about her shoulders like a silky chocolate waterfall. It fell forward over her face when she tilted her head, and she tossed it back over her shoulder with a frown.

"You're the new girl," he said cautiously.

She held out her hand the way he'd seen his dad do when he struck a deal with someone. "Charlie Morrow. And you're Justin McGee."

Suspicion instantly gripped him but he tamped it down. Of course she knew who he was; it was a small town. That didn't mean she was asking about him or anything.

Because he didn't want some girl asking about him.

"You wanna see mine?"

Justin blinked. "Your what?"

"My volcano." A grin burst across her face, making her eyes seem to dance with glee. "I made one, too!"

No! *She* was the competition?

"Uh... sure." He shrugged, his mind working a mile a minute. Being friendly was the best way to compare her project to his without anyone realizing what he was doing.

He followed her to the far end of the long table, checking out the other entries as they walked.

Wally Blackstone had taken apart an engine to show how one was built. One of the Pickens brothers had set up a series of four trays, each holding a wet sponge. One sat under an infrared heat lamp, and another had a small fan blowing across it. A third had both a lamp and a fan. The fourth had nothing. A sign taped to the front of his display read: *Does evaporation happen faster with heat or with wind?*

"I should have a sign," he mumbled, then double-timed it to catch up with Charlie.

Chocolate silk hair swished as she glanced over her shoulder. "You don't need a sign, but I can help you make one if you want. Are you showing how pressure makes a volcano erupt?"

"Uh... sort of how lava flows and covers everything." He didn't want to tell her too much until the judging.

"I'm showing how pressure builds and causes eruptions." She stopped in front of her display and smiled. "And how different volcanos have different kinds of eruptions."

Justin set his empty box of baking soda on the table and took a closer look.

Her volcano didn't have dinosaurs, he noted as a sense of satisfaction crept over him. But her trees and bushes were made from real twigs and pine boughs. And her boulders were real stones, like from the playground. They'd both used scrap pieces of plywood for a base, and they'd both made the volcano out of papier-mache. A smile pulled at his mouth. His volcano looked a little better. Hers was kind of sloppy and haphazard and some of the gray paint had been spread thin so the edges of the paper showed through. Still, her project was going to prove stiff competition. He'd be lucky to win.

She bent and reached into a crate beneath the table, coming up with a familiar yellow-orange box and a blue loose-leaf notebook. "I'm using this and adding vinegar and liquid dish soap. My mom gave me red food coloring so the lava will look real."

Food coloring! Why hadn't he thought of that? His lava would only look like creeping white foam. "What does dish soap do?"

"It makes the bubbles thick." Putting her box of Arm & Hammer down on the table, she squinted at him. "Don't you have something to make it look thicker?"

"Sure I do," he blustered, his mind already plotting and planning. What could he use to thicken and color the mixture?

"Okay." Charlie opened her notebook. "What do you want your sign to say?"

"Um, I dunno." He scanned the room. People were starting to arrive for the demonstrations and the judging. He had to find a way to get away from her so he could figure out how to fix his project. His gaze fell on the lavatory doors. He could say he had to go!

Gross. No, he wouldn't do that.

"Um... I just remembered I have to help Mr. Zajac with... um, something."

Before she could answer, he picked up his box of baking soda and fled the gymnasium.

Bypassing Mr. Zajac's science classroom, he raced down the hallway until he came to Mrs. Bonner's art class. Of course! He was bound to find something in there to add color to his fake lava. After casting a quick glance up and down the hall and seeing no one about, he turned the handle and slipped into the classroom.

The overhead lights were off but sunshine streamed through the windows as he scoured the shelves, looking for something red. Boxes of crayons, colored pencils, trays of water color paints. He paused at those but then shook his head. It would take too much effort and time, soaking the dried chunks of red to turn them into liquid.

His eyes fell on quart-sized jars on an upper shelf. Tempra paint! Already liquid. And it was a thick liquid! Even better. He grabbed two bottles, one red and one orange. He'd use some of both and maybe it would swirl together and come out two-toned. He shoved the box of baking soda into his jacket pocket and carried the jars of paint out of the room and down the hallway. If anyone asked, he'd say he had permission to get the paint, that he needed it to do touchups on his project.

His smile grew wider with each step. He was going to have the best volcano ever.

No one stopped him in the hall. In fact, no one paid him any attention. He arrived in the gymnasium and went straight to work on his project. Charlie had taped a sign to the front.

How an erupting volcano swallows the land and everything on it.

After he set the paint down on the table, he pulled the baking soda from his pocket and emptied it into the bean can reservoir. Then he reached into the grocery bag and pulled out the jug of vinegar. He poured some of the red paint into the jug and instantly it turned the contents red. He added some orange but the two colors only mixed to make an orange-red.

Chewing his lip, he considered the problem. Too bad he couldn't get the lava to come out in chunks.

Hey, why not?

If he dripped some paint in on top of the baking soda, it was so thick it probably wouldn't mix, at least not before he demonstrated his project. By the time the fake lava was rolling down the mountain, it wouldn't matter if it mixed. He drizzled a fair amount of each color into the reservoir, hoping the vinegar would still hit the baking soda and cause a reaction. He stared at the shopping bag with his supplies. Maybe he should add the baking soda from his spare box, just to start it off.

As he dumped the white powder in, anticipation built. This was going to be so cool! He collected the paint jars and shoved them into his paper bag, and then collected the two empty orange boxes and headed for the rolling garbage can. As he deposited his trash, a flash of yellow-orange caught his eye. Another box of baking soda. Probably Charlie's.

Justin looked over toward her diorama but she was nowhere to be found. A bell sounded, and the principal got on stage to announce that all participants should stand near their project and be ready to answer questions, then conduct their demonstration. With a shrug, Justin hurried over to his display. He'd catch up with Charlie after the judging.

After I win.

The judges started with the first graders, who had set up their displays on a table just inside the gym door. It ran at a right angle to the upper elementary students' table and formed the short leg of a giant L. He hadn't bothered to scope out any of their projects since they weren't competing with him, but from his vantage point across the room, he could make out two solar systems and something with magnets.

Finally the group of five judges moved on to the long table. Charlie was up first. He strained to hear what she was saying but only caught the rise and fall of her melodic voice as she made her presentation. She used her hands a lot, pointing to various things on her volcano. Then with a flourish, she poured her cup of colored vinegar into a funnel that led to a tube behind the volcano.

Why hadn't he thought of that? He'd just planned on pouring his in from the top, but lava was formed underground.

Stupid!

A collective sigh and then quiet murmuring rose from the other end of the table, but he couldn't see what had just happened. Surely if her volcano had been as spectacular as she'd built it to be, they would be more impressed.

But with shakes of their heads, the judges moved on to the next project. One gray-haired gentleman — Justin thought it was Mr. Peterson, the high school chemistry teacher — tapped Charlie on the shoulder and said something to her.

She nodded, but she looked very upset. Was she crying?

He had no time to mull over the matter as the judges moved fairly rapidly down the line, and before he knew it, they were standing in front of him.

"Ah... ah, one kind of volcanic eruption shoots out lava," he began, suddenly overcome by nerves. "Lava can be slow or, um, fast. But it cannot be stopped. It swallows and destroys everything in its path. Hawaii — the Hawaiian Islands were made by volcanic activity, and Mount Kilauea was asleep for about eighteen years from 1934 to 1952, but it has been erupting off and on since 1952, with a big eruption in 1959." He paused and drew a deep breath.

At the front of the crowd, Charlie caught his eye and smiled. Her eyes were red. *So she was crying.* Something must have gone wrong at her display.

Justin forced his attention back to his own project, unwilling to think about why he felt badly for her. "I'm, um, going to show you how lava swallows everything in its path."

He picked up his cup of reddened vinegar and poured it into the opening in the volcano's top. They waited.

The audience shuffled their feet.

The judges shuffled their feet.

One judge coughed.

A bit of pale crimson foam bubbled up to the rim and began spilling over the edge and down the sides of the volcano. Elation at his success rose, and Justin allowed himself a proud grin.

The foaming grew stronger, and a blob of orange slid up and over, looking a little less like lava and more like brightly colored phlegm. That was followed by several more slimy globules of red and orange.

Gross!

The volcano looked like it was hocking bloody loogies. More foam welled until the volcano was spewing white and gray froth with streaks of bubbles and slime from its top.

The flow quickly engulfed the dinosaurs and foliage he'd placed so meticulously. Then it inched toward the edge of the board and oozed onto the table.

"Son? Can you turn that off now?" asked Mr. Moss, the principal, shuffling backward a bit just as the foam plopped onto the floor in giant gooey gobs.

Justin glanced around, frantic for anything to stem the stream of red and orange foam. A fistful of paper towels was pressed into his hand, and he looked up to catch Charlie's encouraging smile. They worked together mopping up the mess, but it was no use. More fake lava coursed over the edge and onto the floor, but at least they were able to prevent it from going any farther.

Finally the dripping slowed and came to a stop.

The judges all seemed to sigh at the same time.

"Good demonstration, son," said the white-haired teacher, clapping him on the back. "Maybe try to use a little less solution next time so it doesn't get away from you." He glanced at Charlie, his face lit in a warm smile. "You two should work together. He could have used a little less sodium bicarbonate, and you needed a little more. It's all in the measurements. But you two'll get it right next time."

Perplexed, Justin angled a look at Charlie. "What did he mean by—?"

Galoop.

The sound had come from the volcano. Justin and Charlie turned.

Galoop, gloog, hiss.

"What the heck?" Mr. Peterson stepped closer to the display, a frown creasing his forehead.

Glug.

With a metallic rattle, the volcano started to vibrate. Then it burped and foam exploded from the top, sending orange and red goo several feet in the air.

Mr. Peterson's eyes widened as the volcano's projectile vomit arced and took a downward turn. Charlie squealed and pulled Justin back as the first balls of frothy paint hit the gymnasium floor with a *splat.*

Without the benefit of a guardian angel, Mr. Peterson simply stared in horror as he was pelted with volcanic puke. Red and orange streaked his white hair, and one giant splotch landed on his left cheek then slowly trailed downward.

* * *

Justin finished speaking and scooped the last bite of lasagna onto his fork. Charlie sighed. He'd told it so well, it was almost like he'd transported them back to that horrible day. He'd remembered things even she hadn't.

"Dad!" From across the table, Sean glared. "You totally stole her baking soda, didn't you?"

Justin's lips twisted into a sheepish grin. "Yep, I did. Not intentionally, mind. I didn't remember dumping my first box into the reservoir."

"Who won?" asked Ryan.

An easy grin took over Justin's face. "Leo Pickens with his evaporation experiments."

Justin had been pretty candid in his admission about wanting to win. Had he really felt so intimidated by her? All Charlie could remember was wanting to impress the cutest boy in the class. A giggle slipped out. "We were crazy back then, so serious about the most trivial things." Shooting him a wink, she snagged the last lonely roll from Justin's plate.

"Hey! That's mine." Halfheartedly, he grabbed for it, but she held it out of his reach.

"Give me a break, old man. No way do you have room for this *and* a piece of my pie."

Sandy stood and began gathering empty plates. When Mel and Charlie pushed their chairs back, she waved them off. "Sit still. I have a routine."

"So how does the science fair connect to Christmas?" Ricky handed up his plate when Sandy passed behind him.

"Well, it didn't take us long to figure out what had happened," answered Justin, handing his plate up to Sandy as she paused next to his chair. "I told Charlie how sorry I was."

"And I wouldn't forgive him," finished Charlie. She pushed away from the table and walked over to the coffee maker next to the sink. As Sandy loaded the dishwasher, Charlie put on a fresh pot to brew. "I'll tell the rest in the living room while we have our dessert."

Fumbling around as she arranged items in the dishwasher, Sandy jerked upright and stared, still clutching the lasagna pan in one hand.

Oh, good grief. Look at me, acting like the lady of the house here. "Or... that is, if it's okay with our hostess?" Charlie held her breath and willed the flames to leave her cheeks.

"Of course it is!" A warm smile lit up Sandy's face, and she gave Charlie a one-armed shrug. "I just never thought of it, but that'll be perfect." She set the pan on the bottom rack. "Everyone, grab your choice of dessert here, and we'll go get comfortable."

And so, with a scraping of chairs on the tile, the masses scrambled toward the array of sweets lined up on the counter.

Chapter Twelve

In the living room, as everyone rearranged the pillows and cushions around the sofa where Justin sat, Sandy held an extra large slice of lemon meringue pie just out of reach. With a wink, she pointed to the unhealthy double measure of spray whipped cream. "Promise after the holiday you'll follow your diet again, okay?"

"Yeah, yeah," he grumbled, reaching for the plate. "Just give me the pie."

Standing in the doorway watching it all, Charlie experienced a sharp pang in her heart that she was afraid might be jealousy. She wanted to be the one to settle Justin in his seat, to hand him his pie and give him too much whipped cream. To extract promises he'd take care of himself.

She'd never been prone to jealousy before, but already she'd clenched her jaw and ground her teeth and bitten her tongue trying to stave off those very feelings. Maybe coming out to stay over the holiday hadn't been such a good idea after all.

Justin caught her eye and patted the sofa next to him. "Well? Come on. The young'uns are a-waitin' to hear the rest of the story."

Charlie's heart actually skipped a few beats at the warmth in his eyes. Her insides turned to mush. *Be careful, girl. It's only Justin. Your friend.*

But some warnings were destined to be ignored. She smiled back as she dodged toddlers and teens and cushions and made her way across the room. Sitting next to him had never felt more right.

* * *

Winter in Orson's Folly wasn't much different from winter in Laramie. Layers and layers of clothing had to be worn to go from home to school and then back again. Mittens came off and got shoved into her pockets. Then Charlie unwound the bulky hand-knit scarf from around her neck and hung it on the hook in the coat room. She jammed her hat into one sleeve of her jacket and hung the hot pink down parka over the scarf.

"Hi, Charlie," came Justin's voice from behind her.

She froze. How dared he talk to her? Hadn't she made it perfectly clear that she didn't want to talk to him ever? Well, she would have no trouble reminding him again. She snatched up her loose-leaf binder along with her math and social studies books and whirled about, staring daggers into his eyes. "What do *you* want, McGee?"

"The Christmas Social is this Friday night." The engaging grin on his face and the array of faded freckles sprinkled across his nose might have made her heart melt if she hadn't been so pissed off at him for ruining her chances of winning a ribbon at the science fair. One of the fluorescent lights overhead flickered, and tiny white highlights danced over the shock of blond hair that fell across his eyes.

Because she wanted to brush the hair back off his face, Charlie scowled and locked her arms around her books. "So?"

"So... I wondered if you'd like to go with me." He dropped his gaze and dragged the pointed toe of one boot along a line in the tile. "It can be fun. They have good food, and music, and..."

His voice faded under her narrow-eyed glare.

"No, thanks." Charlie turned and stalked away. Only when she got to the door did she realize she'd stalked in the wrong direction. Her desk was on the other side of the room. Just the thought of hearing him snicker at her mistake made her pause and dart her gaze around. How could she save face?

Other students were already at their desks. She had to do something soon or she'd look stupid — probably already did look stupid, and it was all Justin McGee's fault.

Her eyes lit on the gray pencil sharpener hanging on the wall next to the door. She set her books on the nearby counter, then dug through her pencil case inside the loose-leaf notebook and took out her pencil — her lucky pencil, the yellow one with *DIXON TICONDEROGA No. 2 SOFT* printed on it in shiny green. She jammed it in the sharpener and turned the crank.

After only one turn, the crank jammed. When she attempted to pull her pencil out, it wouldn't budge. She tugged. Jiggled. Pulled again.

Her heart jumped into her throat. Heat invaded her face. She just knew if she turned around, the whole class would be watching her battle with the pencil sharpener.

A shadow filled the doorway, and the soft tones of Mrs. Hunter's voice talking to someone in the hallway reached Charlie's ears. She was out of time.

"I'll show it to you at lunch," said Mrs. Hunter. Then she stepped into the room and pulled the door shut behind her. "Okay, class, take your seats and put your books under your desk, and let's get this math test out of the way."

Charlie tried to turn the sharpener's crank again. When it still didn't move, she grabbed her pencil and yanked hard.

Snap!

The pencil came out of the jammed sharpener. At least half of it did. She stared at the stub of yellow in her hand, at the shiny green lettering, which now simply read *2 SOFT*.

Dismay filled her stomach with dread as, trembling, she struggled for her next breath. *No! Not my lucky pencil!*

"Charlotte, please take your seat and prepare for the math test," urged Mrs. Hunter.

"But... my pencil..." She held up the pathetic remnant.

A few giggles and snickers rose before the teacher quelled them with a glare.

"Do you have a spare?" asked Mrs. Hunter. Clearly she didn't understand the importance of a lucky pencil.

With a heavy sigh, Charlie nodded. "Yes, ma'am." She collected her books and shuffled over to her seat. Justin McGee stared at her the whole way. She knew because she watched him doing it out of the corner of her eye.

Anger welled. She had lost the science fair. And now her lucky pencil had been murdered by the pencil-eating sharpener.

And it was *all* Justin McGee's fault!

She took her seat and opened her notebook to look for another pencil. All she had were two pens, a pink eraser, and a half-pencil with a broken point. She was about to raise her hand to tell Mrs. Hunter when someone dropped a pencil on her desk. It wasn't a Dixon Ticonderoga. It wasn't even yellow. It was an ugly green, and etched in silver were the words *Blackstone's Auto Repair ~ Make a point to get an oil change!* The eraser had never been used and the point was freshly sharpened.

Charlie looked up, ready to show her gratitude for whoever had just rescued her. The words died in her throat when she looked into Justin McGee's smiling face.

She wanted to stab him in the hand with the stupid thing. But she needed the pencil to take the test.

"Thanks," she mumbled, then quickly looked away.

It wasn't her lucky pencil, and it had come from *him*, so she'd probably flunk the test, but at least she would be able to take it and would draw no further attention to herself from the rest of the class. But she would return it the very second she finished.

Or at least when the class ended.

But then something strange happened. The test actually went smoothly. She understood every question, and she was able to work out the problems and get the answers fairly quickly.

Maybe... she would forget to return the pencil, at least for a little while. Until she got the test back to see how she'd really done.

Right before lunch, Mrs. Hunter handed back their tests. "You all did excellent work. I think you've all got a good handle on the decimal system."

Charlie stared wide-eyed at the giant red *100%* written at an angle just beneath her name. Even with her lucky pencil, the highest grade she'd ever gotten on a math test was a *95%*. Maybe she'd hold onto the pencil just a little longer. At least until Justin McGee asked for it back.

But just because he'd loaned her a pencil and she'd done well on a test didn't mean she'd forgiven him for the science fair.

And she would not — ever — go to the Christmas Social at the Orson's Folly Community Center with him.

The next day, she hurried through shucking her coat and hat so as not to run into Justin in the coat room. When she entered the classroom and slipped into her seat, she found a giant candy cane on her desk. Tied to the candy with a green ribbon was a folded piece of red paper. Cautiously, she unfolded the paper and peeked at the note.

I'm sorry. Please come to the Christmas Social with me.
JM

Oh! Would he never give up? She loved candy canes. But now he'd ruined even that by giving her one. She opened her binder and stuffed it into her pencil case then flipped the notebook shut.

Just in case he was watching, she swiveled in her seat and looked back. And there he was, grinning at her.

"No! Go away!" she mouthed silently, and then she turned around and stared at the spotlessly clean blackboard.

The next day was Wednesday, two days before the Christmas Social. Charlie found herself skulking into the classroom, first scoping out her desk in case Justin McGee had left another offering.

But nothing was there. Good. Maybe he'd given up.

She frowned.

All through Mrs. Hunter's lecture about comma placement, Charlie wanted to turn around and see what

Justin McGee was doing. But if she did that, he might think she liked him or something.

And she was still super mad about the science fair.

During library time, Charlie chose *On the Banks of Plum Creek* and *The Long Winter*, both by Laura Ingalls Wilder. She'd only read each of them a couple of times before, but they would be perfect to read again over the Christmas vacation. She walked to the end of the bookshelves, and as she rounded the corner, she ran smack into Justin McGee.

"Are you following me?" she demanded.

He snorted. "No. I'm checking out books, same as you." He held up his choices, *The Phantom Tollbooth* and *A Wrinkle in Time*. Then without another word, he stalked off as though *she* had offended *him*.

Good. Maybe that meant he'd leave her alone.

After the library, it was time to go to the cafeteria for lunch. Chattering and laughter bounced unchecked off the walls as Charlie stood in line waiting for a hot lunch. The cafeteria doubled as the gymnasium, so just returning there was like returning to the scene of Justin McGee's crime. She clenched her jaw and tried to forget what he'd done.

Glowering at his back as he stood in line ahead of her, Charlie waited to hand over her fifty cents in return for a tray from the lunch lady. Her mouth watered at the sight of the white-frosted cupcake on a small plate in the corner. The spaghetti smelled okay but that cupcake would be hard to ignore before the end of the meal.

Sylvia Sanders followed Charlie over, set her own tray on the picnic-style table, then climbed over the seat and sat. "Where did you get the cupcake?"

"It was on my lunch tray," answered Charlie. "Didn't you get one?" A glance around the table revealed no one had a cupcake except her. A frown pinched her forehead. She lifted the plate and gasped.

A familiar-looking piece of red paper lay folded underneath.

Charlie narrowed her eyes and swung her gaze around the room, finally spotting Justin McGee sitting at a table with about a half dozen other boys. His head popped up and he caught her staring at him. Before she looked away, he shot her a grin. Then he turned to speak with Todd Mitchell.

No! He turned away first!

Good grief, how had she let *that* happen? Now he'd think she was always looking for him and staring at him.

Pressing her lips together, she snatched up the folded paper and opened it to read his note.

I'm really, really, REALLY sorry. Please come to the Christmas Social with me. JM

"Not a chance, Justin McGee," muttered Charlie.

"What did you say?" asked Sylvia.

"Nothing." Charlie shook her head and picked up the cupcake. "I was just talking to myself." She should toss the dumb thing in the trash. But it smelled *so* good...

As they were putting on their coats at the end of the day, she found herself alone in the coat room with the object of her anger. He was seated on the bench, gearing up for the bus ride home. Textbooks and a black loose-leaf binder sat next to him. The vinyl on the notebook was cracked and peeling, showing layers of pressed cardboard beneath.

"Stop giving me things," she blurted, planting her hands on her hips.

He finished buckling one of his clunky black snow boots and then looked up. "I just want you to know how sorry I am."

"I *know* how sorry you are." She rolled her eyes. "The whole school *knows* how sorry you are."

"So will you forgive me?" Hope sparked in his clear blue eyes.

"I— No!" Charlie stomped her foot. "I already told you I will never, ever forgive you for what you did. You could write that you're sorry in blood across my front yard and I will never forgive you. *Ever.*"

The hope faded, and Justin offered a shrug before he bent over and fastened the buckle on his other boot.

"Just stop... stop giving me things. I don't want to go to the social with you."

When he didn't answer, didn't even look up, Charlie whirled about and marched away from him. When her bus was nearly to her house, she reached for her books on the seat next to her. Only when she didn't find them did she remember she had left them sitting on the bench in the coat room.

Great. Now, because of Justin McGee, she wouldn't get her homework done.

After dinner, which she barely tasted, she was halfheartedly helping her mom with the dishes when the doorbell rang.

"Who on earth's coming by at this time of the night?" asked Mavis Morrow. "Mike? Can you get the door?"

"On my way," answered Charlie's father.

Mystified herself, Charlie started to join him, but her mother pulled her back. "Just stay here, let your father see to it." She gave Charlie a little push toward the sink. "Hurry up and finish so you can get to your homework."

The white frothy soap bubbles only reminded Charlie of the failed science experiment, further darkening her mood. She picked up a handful and scowled at them.

"Now, what's that look for?" snapped her mom.

Charlie shook the bubbles off her hand and into the sink. "This just reminds me of the science fair that Justin McGee wrecked."

Mavis made an impatient noise. "Not that still. Lands, you need to get over yourself, girl. He explained that it was an accident, said he was sorry. What do you want from him? Blood?"

A chill raced up Charlie's spine. No way did her mother know she had mentioned just that to Justin. Charlie cast a sideways glance at Mavis. *Creepy.*

"Charlotte," called her father in his sternest voice. "Will you come in here, please?"

Uh-oh. Maybe they *did* know. Moving as slowly as she could, Charlie dried her hands and set the towel down, and then she tiptoed into the living room.

And there stood Justin McGee, over near the front door. He wore a denim jacket and clutched a gray Stetson in one hand. In his other hand, he held her loose-leaf notebook, her math book, and her library books.

"You left these in the coat room," he said softly. "My mom had Gus drive me here so I could drop them off."

Charlie could only stare. The cuckoo clock next to the fireplace went off. The little bird popped out seven times and finally stopped. Still, Charlie said nothing.

"Well?" asked her father.

"Thank you," she mumbled, staring at the moss green carpeting.

"I believe Justin has something to show you, Charlotte," said her father. "You'll need your coat. It's outside."

She jerked her head up and her gaze collided with Justin's. An instant grin widened his mouth. Without a word, she grabbed her jacket off the coat tree behind the door. Then she followed her father and Justin out onto the front porch. A string of Christmas lights outlined the roof of their house and cast a colorful glow over the sparkling snow on the ground.

A battered truck sat running in their driveway. The tip of a cigarette glowed orange as the driver took a puff. *Ick.*

Her father tapped her on the shoulder and pointed to the scores of low mounds spread over her front yard. Each one oozed red foam, and they were arranged to spell out a message.

Sorry, Charlie! Please come to the social with me.

"Oh, good gracious!" squealed Mavis as she joined them on the porch. "What is that?"

"It's apparently a message for our daughter," said Charlie's father in a dry tone. "Though it does look as though our yard is hemorrhaging to death."

Charlie gulped. It *did* look like blood. Her gaze flew to Justin. "That's not... that's not real blood, is it?"

"Naw..." He looked away. "It's baking soda and vinegar colored with Tempra paint." Abruptly, he swung his gaze back to her. "So will you please forgive me?"

Charlie looked up at the stars and blew out a long breath. What could she say? If she refused, he'd only keep trying. "Yes."

"Thank you! And..." He sent a sly grin in her direction. "...will you come to the social?"

How could she say no when he once again looked so hopeful? Besides, he had saved her with the pencil and by bringing out her books. And he'd given her candy and cake.

She let out another gusty sigh. "All right. But don't think this means I'm your girlfriend."

Justin's eyes went wide and he took a couple of steps back. "What? No. It's just an invitation to a party. Geez. Ew."

And with that he took off across the front yard. But he paused with his hand on the truck's door handle. "See ya at school tomorrow."

* * *

Justin chuckled as Charlie finished the story. He hadn't been that gawky kid in a while... and yet recently with Charlie he'd gone back to feeling awkward and unsure. A man shouldn't have to go through that stage twice in a lifetime.

"Did the two of you ever officially date?" Sandy reached up and plucked a candy cane from the tree and pitched it to Charlie.

Justin glanced at Charlie and caught her look. "A couple of times. A group of us mostly just hung out together. But we shared a... ahh... a dance or two, didn't we?"

A sweet rosy pink tinted Charlie's cheeks. "How about you, Sean?" she asked quickly. "Do you have a memorable Christmas?"

Sean and Mel exchanged a glance and giggled.

Ryan snorted. "Probably the Christmas they spent in his pickup."

"We did not spend Christmas in Sean's pickup!" squeaked out Mel indignantly.

"Actually, I was thinking of last year." Sean patted the back of Mel's hand. "We both wanted to make Christmas super special for Mitchell, being it was his first. So we each rented a Santa suit and tried to surprise him."

Mel giggled again. "It's a good thing he's too little to remember having two Santas stumbling into each other in his bedroom!"

"Or maybe three," added Sean. "We never did figure out where that rocking horse came from."

Feeling a pair of eyes on him, Justin looked up to find Ricky watching him with a speculative glance. Oh, boy. That wouldn't do. His youngest was bound to figure out more than he should and blow his cover.

"What about you, Natalie?" he asked quickly.

Chapter Thirteen

Something was up. Charlie knew her old friend better than he knew himself. And he'd changed the subject on Sean and Mel far too quickly. Was he perhaps Santa number three? Well, she'd cover his ass and go with the subject change. Plenty of time later to figure out his reasons.

"Yes, Natalie." Charlie crossed one leg over her knee and sat back. "What Christmas sticks out for you?"

"Oh..." Natalie giggled. Obviously it had been easier for her to read from Greta's journal "I guess maybe when I was five and my, um, my..." Her eyes flickered in Mel's direction. "...my parents bought me my first pony. They finally trusted me to ride on my own, but they said I had to take care of my own horse. I soon found out that horses are a lot of work, but I really love it."

"When did you get into barrel racing?" asked Sandy. Bless her, she was obviously trying to help the teen feel more comfortable in her extended family.

"Well, I started it on my own with my pony Jinx. But she really wasn't a racer. When Da— um, Dad saw how much I loved it, and how well I had trained Jinxy, he took me to some rodeos and we talked with some people. I started lessons when I was about seven."

Mel scooted over to kneel in front of Natalie. She touched her on the knee and gazed into her face. "Honey, I may have given birth to you, but your parents are the Carters. I'm okay with that." She swallowed hard. "More than okay, actually. I'm so grateful Hugh found you and that they took you in and loved you." A tear fell unchecked. "I love you, but don't ever think you have to hide that you love your parents, okay?"

Natalie's face lit brighter than the gleaming Christmas tree. "Thank you," she whispered, and flung her arms around Mel's neck.

Sandy cleared her throat and nodded toward the hearth. Bethany had crawled into the dog's bed and was curled up with Punkin, while Patch watched over them both. "We need to get these kiddos to bed."

"Yep." Mel gave Nattie one last squeeze then stood and retrieved Mitchell from underneath the Christmas tree. "And then we have to get the boots set out."

"The boots?" asked Natalie, confusion drawing creases across her brow as she glanced between Mel and Sandy.

Justin chuckled. "Santa doesn't fill stockings in this house. He fills boots."

"Really...?" Charlie shifted so she could see Justin's face. Were they pulling a joke? "And I suppose there's a story behind that?"

A playful grin put laughter in his eyes. "Nothing so complicated. When the boys were young, they got sent to bed early when we caught them rifling through Christmas packages, tearing the corners and trying to figure out what was in them." He stared at Ryan and raised one eyebrow.

Ryan squirmed a little and averted his gaze toward the Christmas tree.

"Their stockings were still in their bedrooms, waiting to be officially hung. So Beth suggested using their boots instead." He laughed, gleeful and infectious. "That year, I'll tell ya... if I'd had coal, those boots would have been filled to the brim."

Beth...

Charlie forced her smile to remain in place; she could only hope no one noticed how stiff it had suddenly become.

"Well, we can only hope our little one isn't as rambunctious as her daddy," said Sandy softly from the doorway. She nodded at Mitchell, still sleeping in Sean's arms — and clutching the red Christmas ball from the tree tightly in one fist. "We already know that one has his daddy's tenacious spirt."

Mel pried the ornament from her son's fingers. "That's what worries me. If he's already like this, what will he be like in fifteen years?"

As the young parents left the room with their sleeping toddlers, Charlie pushed to her feet and walked to the window.

"I'm kind of tired myself. I think I need to turn in," whispered Natalie. Something thumped on the floor. "Where do I put my boot?"

"Over here," said Ricky, as plates clinked and clattered.

Charlie watched their interaction in the window's reflection as Ricky cleared the remnants of dessert from the hearth and made room for Natalie's boot. Each threw covert glances at each other, and neither seemed to notice the budding interest. So long as they took things slowly, it would be fun to watch young love in bloom.

After placing a shy goodnight kiss on Justin's cheek, Natalie picked up the plates Ricky hadn't been able to carry and the two left, giggling at something between themselves.

And then there were two.

Charlie stepped closer to the window, blocking the reflection behind her as she peered out into the night.

Moonlight poked through lacy gray clouds that writhed in the sky. A stiff wind bent the row of pines lining the top of the drive, and that same wind had piled snowdrifts over the drive Walt had plowed earlier.

It didn't look to Charlie like she would be going home any time soon. Maybe in a couple of days. And that was just fine with her so long as she kept it real. She and Justin were friends — always had been, always would be. If it never progressed to anything more, she could live with that.

Beth had been gone a long time. He'd raised their boys on his own. She didn't think he'd even dated since her death. And she wasn't jealous of Beth, not really. After all, Charlie had been married, too, and she'd been crazy in love with Henry.

If only widowhood wasn't so damn lonely.

But it was more than that, and Charlie knew it. A part of her heart had always belonged to Justin. Ever since she'd watched his mortified expression as he'd explained about accidentally taking her box of baking soda and thinking it was his.

But maybe their time had passed. They *had* both married other people. Or perhaps their feelings had never really been meant to deepen into something more.

Strong arms slipped around her from behind. Despite her muddled thoughts on the subject, when Justin drew her against him and leaned his chin on her shoulder, Charlie's body reacted in a fairly predictable manner, with tingles and hot darts of emotion that flew through her and pooled in her stomach, where they woke up a flurry of butterflies.

She pressed the side of her head against his and sighed.

"You look like you have some deep thinking going on over here," he murmured.

"Not so deep, really," she said.

"Liar," he whispered.

And then he was turning her to face him, fitting her intimately into his embrace, resting one hand on her hip while the other lifted to cup her cheek. Then he bent and pressed a gentle kiss to her lips, slow and lingering.

And utterly devastating.

The fluttering in her middle exploded into a thousand flaming fireflies, zooming, zinging, bursting with even more heat.

She parted her lips.

And he took the invitation, exploring with his tongue, sucking on her lower lip. Fine tremors shot through her, weakening her knees.

Who'd-a thought?

He eased back and nodded upward toward the ceiling. "Sandy hung mistletoe everywhere."

She followed his gaze and spotted... nothing. Mistletoe? After a world-rocking, toe-curling kiss, he was jabbering about mistletoe that wasn't even there? Why? Unless he wanted to give her an out if she desired one.

The only thing she desired was... him.

Hope sprang to life. "That didn't feel like a mistletoe kiss."

Slowly he shook his head. "It wasn't." He turned them slightly so the glow from the Christmas tree illuminated them both. For just an instant, in the twinkling and shadowing playing over his face, she saw the ten-year-old boy she'd put off so many times, yet he'd kept coming back. And then she caught the earnest warmth of the man he'd grown into. "Is that a problem for you?" he asked softly.

"No," she whispered. And then because words no longer seemed adequate — or necessary — she leaned into him and fitted her mouth to his, seeing his tender kiss and raising him to a hot one.

And in a flash he followed suit, plundering, demanding, taking everything she offered, while he held her against him and explored with his hands. Errant thoughts that she was no longer a svelte young woman crept in, but she pushed them aside. If he didn't care, who was she to worry?

When he finally drew back, a crimson flush decorated his face, and his hand trembled as he brushed a strand of hair out of her eyes.

Good to know he was as shaken as she.

* * *

"I... ah... I know we aren't kids anymore." Though he enjoyed watching the way the flashing Christmas lights changed her expression, he needed more, needed to feel more. He dropped his forehead to hers, reveling in the warmth that seemed to reach out to him.

"Neither of us are teenagers any longer, Justin." She chuckled and rubbed her brow back and forth against his. "As enjoyable as life has been, I'm not prepared to return to that awkward stage." An exaggerated shudder chased through her. "Especially not these days."

"I... don't..." ...*know where to go from here.* The speech had come off so well the hundred or so times he'd rehearsed it in his head. He blew out a frustrated breath. "After Beth, I..."

Charlie stiffened and lifted her forehead off his. "Justin..." she choked. "I know... I know how much you loved Beth. I'm not... I'd never..."

"Shh..." He claimed her lips again, slowly and gently, ending by brushing tender kisses at the corners of her mouth. "I know you aren't trying to replace Beth, and I can't possibly take Henry's place. Wouldn't want to. Neither of us would." He spooled one finger into her hair then slowly pulled it free. "We've both been in love before. I never expected to feel this way again, this — this—" He moved his hand and cupped her cheek to stop his shaking. "We're not kids any longer, but when I'm with you... I *feel* like one." He sucked in a long breath then slowly released it. "I can't explain it, but I know Beth would approve. Our lives, our hearts didn't stop when we lost our spouses. And..." He shrugged. "I love you, Charlie. Always have, but it's moved into something... different. Something I want to explore."

There, he'd said it all. Now the ball was in her—

With a tiny cry, she glued her mouth to his, moving her lips back and forth, teasing his lower lip with her tongue. He angled his head and deepened the kiss. As she clutched his waist, somehow finding his most ticklish spot, he gave his hands permission to wander and explore, reveling in her softness, the gentle curves, the way she fit against him. The way her sweet scent filled his nostrils.

A throat cleared and they sprang apart like... like guilty teenagers. Justin suppressed a chuckle.

"Remember, Santa's watching," admonished Ryan. He stood in the doorway, work jacket in hand. "Hey, Sean and Ricky and I are headed for the barn to... ah, check on the stock."

Yeah, Justin had a barn trip of his own to make but he suspected that would have to be in the wee hours of the morning, given how busy the house was. He waved a hand at his eldest son.

"Great, well... don't do anything I wouldn't." Ryan tapped twice on the woodwork and disappeared.

After he was certain they were alone again, Justin smiled. "As my daddy used to say, 'that leaves the field wide open.'" He tugged Charlie back up against him for round two.

Chapter Fourteen

Charlie popped her eyes open. After a second, they adjusted to the ambient light filtering in from outside. With so much snow brightening the world, it was impossible to judge the time, but it felt early. Deep breathing from the twin bed across the room signaled Natalie was still asleep. Charlie rolled over and squinted at the bedside alarm clock.

"Three a.m.," she muttered. What in Sam Hill had awakened her at three o'clock?

A creak came from somewhere out in the hallway, followed by another. Then she caught the sound of whispering. Who on earth was up at such an hour? Had one of the children gotten sick?

Her breath caught. Or Justin?

In a panic, she sat up and swung her feet over the side of the bed. Wouldn't that just be her rotten luck? Finally get things going with Justin and— *No! Don't think of it. Just step into the hallway and see if everything's okay.*

The light drifting in from the yard brightened. One of the floods must have popped on. Charlie stepped over to the window and peeked out.

Two figures trudged across the yard. Their awkward gait and wide trail told her they wore snowshoes. Collarlength hair gleamed like an orange beacon under the floodlight. And she'd recognize that old tan work jacket and worn gray Stetson anywhere. Ricky and Justin. What on earth were they doing up so early? Surely Justin and Ricky didn't see to the stock at such a ridiculous hour.

Charlie turned and studied the jeans and sweater she'd hung over the desk chair the night before, when she'd gotten ready for bed. Should she get dressed and go help out? Why weren't Sean and Ryan helping? Unless they were already out there.

The pair reached the unoccupied bunkhouse and disappeared around the side. Definitely heading toward the barn.

A sudden burst of wind shook the window, sending a chill through Charlie's bones. Shivering, she scurried over to the end of her bed and grabbed her robe. Stepping into her fuzzy slippers on the run, she raced back to the window and took up watch again. If Ricky and Justin didn't return to the house in the next ten or fifteen minutes, she'd get dressed and go find them.

But she didn't have to wait that long. The pair of them reappeared from around the bunkhouse. Ricky was carrying a bulky crate, and Justin pulled a long toboggan loaded down with boxes and bags. The floodlights reflected off the shiny packages.

"Gifts!"

"Mmm?" Natalie stirred and rolled over.

Charlie turned away from the window and froze. In less than a minute, Natalie's deep, even breathing assured she had returned to sleep. By the time Charlie looked out the window again, Justin and Ricky had disappeared in the shadow of the house.

Satisfied that nothing was wrong, Charlie subdued her curiosity and returned to her bed. If Justin had wanted her in on his little secret, he'd have invited her to the middle-of-the-night raid. It was nice to see he still had the ability to surprise her. Filled with thoughts of Justin and his sexy goodnight kisses, Charlie snuggled under the covers with a sigh.

Her eyes popped back open. *I have the perfect gift!*

Flinging off the covers again, she stood and grabbed her purse from the desk chair. It didn't take much digging to find the long slender box in the bottom. Clutching it against her chest, she couldn't stop smiling. It was the perfect way to show Justin how she felt. As long as he didn't think she was crazy for holding onto it for so long.

Creaking footfalls and whispers in the hallway announced the two Santas had made it back upstairs. She waited a little longer until she was certain they must have returned to their bedrooms. Then she cracked the door and peeked into the dimly lit hallway.

Empty.

In just a couple of minutes, she was down the stairs and in the kitchen. She'd seen some extra wrapping paper in the storage room off the kitchen when she'd been baking her pies. Hopefully no one had used it all in the meantime. She opened the door and flipped the switch, and instantly spotted the partial roll of blue paper with tumbling snowmen all over it.

Jackpot!

There wasn't much left, but it was enough. She finished the wrapping job, turned off the light, and headed for the living room. The row of boots on the hearth were filled to overflowing. The little kid inside desperately wanted to go over there and see what was in hers. Justin's boot was easy to spot. Big old man boot, all scuffed and worn into comfort.

She slipped her gift to Justin under the tree near the packages she'd brought along for the children. Casting one last look at the filled boots, she sighed and then crept up the stairs and snuggled back into bed.

The next time she opened her eyes, she had no doubt it was dawn. It was too light in the room to be anything but. A trip to the window revealed fingers of mauve and vermillion clawing their way into a deep turquoise sky. A few scattered stars still winked high in the sky, but as the shiny gleam of white grew on the horizon even those winked out.

Christmas Day!

What were her girls doing? Maybe they'd be home and not too busy to take her calls later. If not, then certainly in the next day or so. She rolled out of bed, not surprised to see Natalie was already awake and gone. The other bed was made up as though it hadn't even been slept in. Charlie grabbed her jeans and sweater and hurried to the bathroom to get dressed. She'd have to go to breakfast in her fuzzy pink cat lady slippers, since one of her boots currently sat on the hearth, lined up with nine others.

Cat! They'd put Punkin up in the laundry room the night before. How had he managed? And he was most likely hungry.

Some cat lady I am.

Voices arose from the sitting room, but the aroma of coffee drew her toward the kitchen. She'd feed Punkin and then grab a cup of java and join the family.

"Thanks for understanding. I'll be waiting." That was Justin. Who was he talking to? "Yeah, urban rescue." He laughed. "Okay, bye now."

A ball of orange fluff tore past without so much as waving a whisker. Looked like they'd have to work on Punkin's social skills. Maybe after she started feeding him regularly, he'd pay more attention to the human who'd just taken him in.

Probably not.

When Charlie entered the kitchen, Justin was busy serving himself a piece of lemon meringue pie. He scooped it up and slid it onto the plate next to his cup of coffee, and then pushed the rest of the pie back in line with the other desserts from the evening before.

When Charlie cleared her throat, Justin gave a guilty little start.

"You're busted, old man." She stepped into the kitchen and located a mug for her coffee. The row of pies did look kind of tasty. And fruit was healthy, right? What could a slice of apple pie hurt? Grinning, she dished up herself a slice of pie.

Just call me a rebel.

"Who were you talking to?" she asked, stirring sugar into her black coffee.

"Talking to?" He blinked at her.

"I heard you talking in here when I came downstairs." She set the lid back on the sugar bowel.

"Huh." He picked up his cup and plate. "Must have been the kitten."

That brought her up short, and she frowned at him. "You talked to the kitten about an urban rescue?"

"Urban rescue?" He shook his head. "I have no idea what you're talking about, woman. Come on." He headed for the living room, leaving her no choice but to follow or start talking to herself.

"Do you know if anyone fed Punkin?" she asked when she caught up with him.

"Actually, three of us did." Justin stepped aside and gestured for her to enter the living room first.

Just as she'd figured, everyone was already there, which made her the rotten egg. Punkin had found an early morning sunbeam and flopped in it, leaving no room in the ray of light for Patch. The dog didn't seem to mind, though. He'd made himself at home in one corner of the sofa.

The tree twinkled and glistened. And there were even more mounds of presents than she'd seen in the middle of the night.

Bethany and Mitchell sat on a plastic tarp eating toast with jam. Good idea. Probably saved on cleaning the rug. They seemed more interested in the food than the presents, and Charlie chuckled. Next year would likely be a different story.

Janet hadn't known what to do about Christmas either until she was about three. Then she had no problem teaching her sisters all the fun to be had on Christmas morning. And there was yet another thought of her missing girls. A sigh slipped out, but Charlie pushed the sadness from her heart and allowed Justin to lead her to the sofa.

"Off the furniture, Patch," he ordered half-heartedly.

The dog stood, stretched, moved over a couple inches, and plopped down again.

"Hey!" complained Justin.

Patch yawned and rolled onto his back.

"That's okay. I think I have room to squeeze in here." Charlie parked herself between Justin and the dog. As they sat thigh-to-thigh, he settled one arm behind her shoulders, and a little charge of awareness raced along her spine.

Sandy stopped dead in the middle of handing Bethany a sippy cup of juice and stared. A slow grin widened her smile, and she nudged Mel.

Always the cheeky one, Mel shot Sandy a grin and a wink, and then she rubbed her thumb over her fingers and mouthed "pay up."

No one rushed to check the overflowing boots or open the packages. Instead, they took their time enjoying the company and the impromptu breakfasts — it seemed pie was a popular choice, though Sandy drew the line at whipped cream.

"Save some for dessert today," she demanded, holding the can behind her back while Ryan encircled her with his arms and tried to snag it. With a squeal, she ducked his embrace and dashed from the room. "I'll be back after I get the turkey in the oven!"

Feeling a bit bold, Charlie turned toward Justin and laid her cheek over his chest. The steady *thump-thump* of his heart was as comforting as it was amazing, considering it had stopped entirely not too long ago.

"Turkey's in," announced Sandy, entering the room about ten minutes later. Charlie sat up again, ready to watch them all dive in to their presents, including the few she'd brought with her.

Mel and Ricky exchanged a glance and a smile, and Mel stood.

"Hey, Mel, I think Mitchell needs a change," said Ricky as he wrinkled his nose.

Natalie sniffed. "I don't—"

"Okay, let me get him squared away." Mel scooped up her son and they left the room.

When Mel returned, Ryan decided Sandy needed her camera, and when he returned with that, Sean announced he was thirsty. It was almost as though they were taking turns delaying the inevitable. How sweet.

But a little frustrating.

A flash of silver and turquoise at Natalie's throat caught Charlie's attention, and she took a closer look. A pretty butterfly crafted in a blueish stone nestled against ivory skin. "Natalie, what a lovely necklace."

The girl held it out so Charlie could get a better look. "Mel gave it to me for my birthday last night. It's my birthstone." She beamed with pleasure as she sat back down.

Justin gazed at Ricky and released a long sigh filled with contentment. He moved his free hand and it almost looked like he gave his son a thumbs-up. Ricky grinned, so some kind of message definitely passed between them.

Finally, everyone was in the room at the same time, with no apparent emergencies. Still, no one made a move to open any presents.

A phone rang and it took a second for Charlie to realize the sound was coming from her pocket. She could have wept with joy when she dug out her phone to see Heather's number flashing on the screen.

"Hello?"

"Mom! Merry Christmas!" Her daughter sounded so happy, Charlie could forgive her not being present for Christmas.

Charlie's spirits soared. "Heather! Sweetie! Merry Christmas! How are you? What are you doing?" Oh, dear, did she ever sound needy! But it was too late to take it back.

"I'm on a sleigh ride. It's so cool! Zoe and Janet are here, too!"

"Oh... that sounds really fun, honey." So the girls had gotten together after all. Well, that was good, at least. Charlie blinked back hot tears. "I wish I could be there with you," she squeezed past the emotion in her throat.

"You can be!" said Heather, laughing.

"I can...?" Confusion stole Charlie's voice. What was she missing?

Justin lifted his arm from her shoulders and stood, pulling her up with him. "Come on. I think your first Christmas present is outside."

Charlie balked. "It's not a message in the snow, is it?"

"Not a message," said Justin with a grin. "But it's in the snow, all right. Come *on*!" He tugged her toward the foyer.

When he swung open the front door, the glare of sun on snow blinded Charlie and she squinted against the brilliance.

Someone laid her coat over her shoulders and she shrugged into the sleeves as Justin led her onto the porch.

An old-fashioned red and black sleigh pulled by two sturdy brown horses was just entering the circular drive in front of the house. Snorting puffs of white, they plodded with little effort through the snow.

Charlie's jaw slackened and she stared as the driver — Colt Ford, of all people! — pulled the sleigh to a stop in front of the house. Her three girls sat in the back, along with her son-in-law, Evan.

"Oh, my! Oh, my!" Tears cascaded from her eyes, down her cheeks, and dripped onto her hands. "I didn't know. When did— *How* did you get here?"

"Justin called day before yesterday and told us all to pack our things and he'd send transportation," said Zoe, beaming. She scrambled from her seat and dropped to the ground, landing knee-deep in white powder. "He said he wouldn't argue and wouldn't accept any excuses."

Charlie frowned. "You came by sleigh from Jackson?"

Janet giggled as she let her husband help her out of the sleigh. "Of course not. A really dishy guy with a helicopter picked us up and got us to Orson's Folly before the storm got bad." She winked at Heather, who dropped the lap blanket onto the seat and stepped out into the snow, taking care to place her feet in her sisters' footprints. "Zoe's crushing on him."

"I am not!" screeched Zoe. "Just because I gave him my number and told him I was free for New Year's..."

"And we stayed at your place last night," added Heather, as though Zoe hadn't spoken. "And Colt got us from there this morning in his four-wheel drive, but the road's blocked from his place on, so he suggested the sleigh ride."

The girls chattered excitedly as they told the story; they sounded deliriously happy. But they couldn't be as happy as Charlie was, just listening to the good-natured teasing.

"Colt? You want to come in for some Christmas dinner?" asked Sandy.

Ryan moved to the rear of the sleigh and unloaded suitcases and a stack of wrapped boxes.

Colt doffed his black hat and gave Sandy a half smile. "Thank you anyway, but my sister's home from college and doing up our own dinner." He glanced over at Sean. "I've gotta pass your place on the way home. I figure I'll look in on your animals for you."

"Thanks!" said Sean, obviously pleased by the kind offer. "You have my cell number if you find anything I need to know about?"

"Sure do. Ma'am. Nice to see you. Hope you all enjoy Christmas." Colt nodded at Charlie and returned his hat to his head.

Oh, she would, she so very much would, now that her babies were there with her.

As Colt left the drive, Justin turned to the group with a grin. "Well, now that everyone's finally here, we've got presents to open."

* * *

The room might have exploded with four extra people being shoehorned into it, but with a bit of shuffling and the desk chair rolled in from the office, they managed. Justin stopped watching the festivities after only a couple of presents. He much preferred to watch Charlie, who had once again taken up a seat next to him. She'd always been lovely and happy, but something had been missing, especially the past couple of days. With the arrival of her family, she'd come alive. It was like her daughters had been the magic spark that gave her life.

They plowed through the boots first, laughing at some of the gag gifts, making faces at practical items like lip balm.

The stack of unopened packages dwindled, and the trash bags filled with old wrapping paper fattened as the pile of new treasures in front of each person grew.

Sandy sent Bethany toddling over with a small, thin box wrapped in snowmen. "Peepaw! Open!" she demanded.

No tag, but his name was written across the paper in familiar block letters. He twisted to raise an eyebrow in query to Charlie.

She shrugged, but her eyes danced with a suppressed smile. Something was tickling her funny bone. Quickly, he opened one end and slipped out a long white box. Using a bit of caution — for this was a gift from Charlie, and she was bursting with merriment — he lifted the lid. There, nestled on a bed of white cotton, was a green pencil, with a pristine eraser. Silver letters crawled along its length.

Blackstone's Auto Repair ~ Make a point to get an oil change!

She'd held onto it. She'd considered it precious and special enough to hold onto. His very first gift to her. Justin burst into laughter.

"It's about time I got this back."

Charlie beamed at him.

* * *

He was laughing. He got it! He understood her message.

"Mom?" Janet tilted her head and regarded Charlie, her lips pursed, forehead creased with concern. "Is everything okay?"

Charlie shook her head. Her children probably thought their old lady was losing her mind. "It's absolutely perfect," she said, exchanging another glance with Justin and smiling.

"This one's for Charlie," said Mel with a giggle. She glanced up from the small package wrapped in green-and-gold striped paper, and wiggled her eyebrows. "From Justin."

Justin stiffened expectantly as Charlie tore off the paper, exposing the yellow-orange box underneath. While her daughters stared at the present with frowns of confusion painted on their faces, Charlie threw back her head and let loose with a hearty guffaw.

"What does the note say?" asked Zoe, leaning forward.

Charlie unfolded the piece of red paper and read out loud. *"Sorry, Charlie! Will you please marry me?"*

She flashed her gaze over to Justin, unable to stop smiling as a mixture of emotions rushing through her.

Returning her smile, he pulled a square red velvet box out of his pocket and lifted the top. A shining heart-shaped diamond set in a wide platinum band winked out at the room.

"Oh..." she breathed. "It's beautiful!" Fine tremors rocked her hand as she reached out and traced the band. She lifted her eyes and their gazes collided with an emotional explosion. There was only one answer to that question. "Yes."

The room erupted in cheers and applause, but Charlie barely heard as she settled into Justin's embrace and lifted her face to receive his tender kiss.

Epilogue

"I'm stuffed." Justin pushed back from the kitchen table and patted his belly. The turkey platter was bare. The side dishes had all been emptied as well. "Not sure I even have room for pie."

Charlie snorted. "Not even pecan pie?"

Justin weighed his sweet tooth against the tightness of his belt, and decided against it. "Nope. Maybe later." He leaned forward and studied Charlie's face. "You happy?"

Tenderness filled her eyes. "Justin McGee." She leaned forward and kissed him hard and fast. "I am happier than you can possibly imagine."

Sandy and Mel stood and began clearing dishes.

Ricky got up as well. "I've gotta go drop hay for the stock."

"Can I help?" asked Natalie, nearly bouncing out of her seat.

"Ah... sure," he answered, seeming a little uncertain.

Ryan and Sean exchanged a glance. "We'll go, too," said Sean. "Get twice the work done in half the time."

The group moved toward the back door.

"Wait!" cried Charlie. "Ricky... you never told us about your favorite Christmas."

Justin held his breath at the potentially loaded question.

"That's easy." Ricky shot Charlie a grin and then settled his gaze on Justin. "My favorite Christmas ever is..." He shrugged. "...this one."

About the Author

Kay Springsteen cannot remember a time when she wasn't telling stories... beginning with her earliest memory from about age 3, when, rather than accept punishment for changing her father's alarm clock and making him late for work, she placed the blame squarely on the pink fuzzy shoulders of her faithful companion, Flopsy, a 10-inch tall stuffed rabbit with satin ears and black thread whiskers. Over the years, her tales have become more creative and a bit less self-serving. The mother of four adult children, she often draws on her own life experiences as well as the experiences of her kids and their spouses for her writing. The kids all know the only way to keep their own lives from being spotlighted is to give up a sibling's sad or funny story. Everything's fair game with Mom. And that all makes for lots of fun in her widely scattered but somehow close-knit family. Find Kay on Facebook and at her blog:

http://kayspringsteen.wordpress.com/

Did you read the first book in the series?

Lifeline Echoes

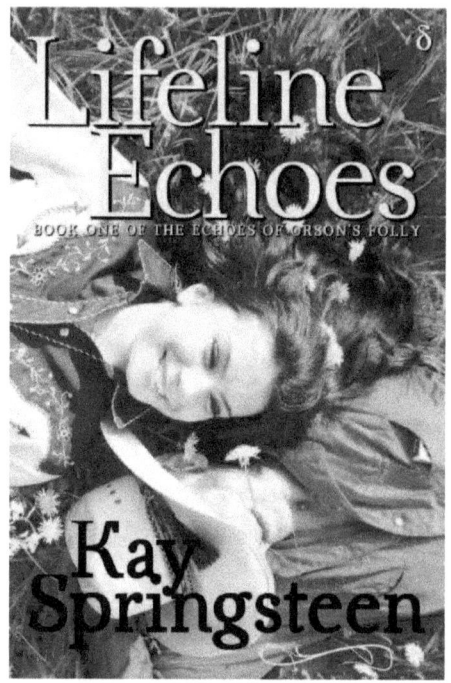

Prologue

There is no natural phenomenon which is held by all mankind in greater dread than earthquakes. Our ideas of permanence, solidity and strength are based upon the condition of the earth, as we daily see it; so that when the firm ground shakes under us, there naturally comes over the mind a feeling of abject helplessness. ~New York Times, April 9, 1872

Seven years earlier...
    Splat.
    "Son of a—"

Sandy glared down at her double chocolate iced mocha. Pale brown slush slid off the toe of one white shoe to form a sticky puddle on the blacktop.

A quick glance at her watch told her she'd have to hurry or she'd be late for her shift as a dispatcher for Los Angeles City Emergency Services. She kicked the melting mush from her shoe and stepped around the puddle of yuck and raced across the parking lot to the low brick building. Behind her, traffic on the packed freeway growled and honked.

Good morning, Los Angeles.

Sandy yanked on the heavy glass door and stepped into the coolness of the air conditioned building with a sigh.

"Morning, Alley Cat!" greeted Rose from behind the reception desk. "Lunch at Del Rio's today?"

"Hi, Rose. Yeah, lunch sounds great. Gotta run. I'm late." With a wave, Sandy hurried past the desk and into the ladies' restroom. She set her oversized purse on the counter and grabbed several paper towels. Crouching, she dabbed at the mush, noting with dismay that it had worked into the seams of her athletic shoes.

"Gross," she muttered. She'd be lucky if it didn't stink like sour milk at the end of her shift. After she mopped off the worst of it, she pushed to her feet and staggered sideways. Her hand hit the cool marble wall of the first stall as she fought to steady herself.

"What the hell?"

A low primeval rumble surrounded her, invaded her midsection and radiated up into her heart and throat. Sandy stumbled to the left then the right. The fluorescent light overhead became a flickering strobe.

Earthquake!

The word registered in the recesses of her mind, and spurred her toward the door. She had to get out of the enclosed space before the ceiling collapsed and buried her.

Sudden blackness swallowed her as the lights lost the battle to stay on. The grumble grew to a roar and then a scream. She lurched to the right, pushed off the wall, and careened through the bathroom door. The scream grew louder before she realized it came from her own mouth. The floor beneath her rolled and writhed as her cries were echoed by a half-dozen coworkers at their workstations. Shelves toppled, notebooks tumbled to the floor.

The roar dwindled to a dull grating, the heaving slowed and finally halted. Sandy lay on her side, her back jammed against the wall. Her insides still quivered and shook like jelly, the remnants of the quake continuing in her viscera. Chills washed over her as she sat up and took stock of the dispatch room. Her coworkers moved slowly, sitting and looking around, dazed expressions gracing their faces.

"Holy cow," murmured Rose, pushing to her feet and doing a three-sixty. "That felt like an eight or a nine."

Fluorescent lights overhead sputtered then half of them winked on. That would be the backup generator, running nonessentials at half power.

More operators pushed to their feet, their faces all wearing uniform dazed expressions. Jabbering filled the air as a dozen people seemed to find their voices at the same time. The cacophony crescendoed. Any second her head would explode. She closed her eyes and attempted to sort out what was being said.

"...my kids..."

"I think my arm's broken..."

"Maybe we should get..."

"Comm's down!" called out Albert Torres, IT wizard and technical problem solving guru. "Switching to backup."

Phones began ringing. Frowning, Sandy oriented herself and located her desk. Someone had to answer the calls. And there would be calls.

She located her station and placed the headset over her ear, then punched the button. "Emergency services—"

A shrill scream came over the line and assaulted her ear. Forcing herself to speak calm words of reassurance as she wrestled open her desk drawer and pulled out an empty notebook and a black pen, Sandy managed to discern that the caller was an elderly woman who was merely disoriented and frightened.

The phone lines began to flash as more calls came in. Around her, more dispatchers followed Sandy's lead and began answering.

"Backup comms are on line," announced Albert, emerging from the computer room.

The first report of a fire came ninety seconds after Sandy started answering calls. The gas line alongside the Convention Center had burst and somehow ignited. Hell had erupted in Central Los Angeles.

Sandy couldn't stop the tremors running along the inner fault lines of her own neural pathways. *I'm a professional. People are depending on me.* She studied the older system that had just been replaced by a two million dollar upgrade, only months earlier, and re-familiarized herself with the buttons and switches. Then, in a voice that only barely trembled, she dispatched Fire Station Number 9 to the L.A. Convention Center.

The first shift after Sandy's vacation was off to a very rocky start. Before that shift was over, she would learn two important things. First, she was getting the hell out of L.A. Second, it was possible to fall in love with someone, sight unseen, in twenty-three hours and fifty-seven minutes.

Chapter One

Present day

Sunny and warm, the perfect day for mourning lost love. Maybe this would be the year she'd finally be ready to move on. Even as the thought teased her, Sandy suspected it might take another cataclysmic event to let go of the man she'd given her heart to in less than a day.

Summer was a handful of days off, but the mountain air was clean and brisk, nothing like the heavy smog of L.A., where she'd first met *him*. She had no memories of the man in this place except for the ones he'd painted into her mind while they'd talked. Yet Wyoming was where she felt his presence.

Her red roan colt pranced beneath her, needing to run off his teenage-intensity energy. Dry dirt kicked up by Domingo muffled the sound of his hoof-falls to dull scuffling *plunks*, which he punctuated with occasional impatient snorts.

As they traveled, the dusty ground became more firmed and flattened. Gray rocky outcroppings thrust upward amid a tan landscape dotted by the washed-out green of desert grasses. More of the same lay between them and the scrub pines along the swell of foothills in the distance.

Sandy pointed Domingo toward those hills, finally allowing the exuberant colt to set his own pace. He catapulted them across the plain, brawny muscles alternately flexing and contracting beneath her, racing at a full gallop. The denim jacket she hadn't bothered to fasten caught the wind and billowed behind her. Chilly air worked icy fingers along the exposed skin of her neck, bringing with it a wonderful ache.

They topped a gentle rise and a sea of yellow and purple wildflowers surprised her, God's own casually sown garden. The sky overhead was deep blue and cloudless. With the prairie behind her and the snow-covered peaks ahead, Sandy pulled Domingo up inside a cathedral of Ponderosa pines, closed her eyes, and inhaled the pungent scent. It was exactly as he had described it, which made it the perfect place to remember him.

Seven years had passed, yet her pain was an exquisite, fresh wound, probably owing to the fact that she revisited the memory once a year on the anniversary of that horrific day. In the hills of Wyoming that he had loved and missed so much, in the place he had brought her to with just his words, Sandy picked the scab off the wound she never quite allowed to heal.

* * *

The job was all that mattered now. Sandy made herself disregard the toppled shelves and scattered books. She blocked out all thoughts about the likely state of her own home. As she listened to the chatter on the official channels, she kept meticulous handwritten notes regarding the status of each unit checking in.

"Battalion 9-Alpha, this is Engine Squad 9-Bravo, do you copy?" The connection was filled with static and the voice was muffled, hard to hear.

Sandy waited for the response of the battalion chief on scene. None came.

The callout was repeated, the voice sounding a bit more urgent. "This is L.A. Engine Squad 9-Bravo, dispatched to the Convention Center—" Again static broke the transmission.

Following protocol, after the second unanswered call, Sandy intervened. "Copy you, ES-9-Bravo. This is central dispatch. Your transmission is breaking up."

She checked her watch and jotted the time in her notes: 0724 hours.

The response was drowned out by a loud burst of static in the earpiece.

"9-Bravo, be advised you are breaking up," she repeated.

More harsh squawks of static burst from the receiver. Sandy winced. If that kept up, her head might explode — or at least an eardrum. Then, amid the static, she clearly heard the code every dispatcher dreaded. "9-Bravo is 10-60, this location. Code three, code three, code three... trapped..."

The code for firefighter down!

Static filled the airwaves again as Sandy punched buttons on her console, frantically trying to boost the signal.

"*Dispatch, are you there?*" The voice was screaming. "*Central! This is 9-Bravo in need of assist. The building's coming down around us!*"

Afraid to switch over to relay, with the risk of losing contact altogether, she motioned to Ellen, the dispatcher sitting next to her. Quickly, Sandy wrote on her notepad in bold black ink: UNIT IN TROUBLE.

At the next desk, Ellen nodded and switched channels to contact the Battalion 9 squad leader over the comm.

"*9-Bravo, this is Central Dispatch,*" Sandy acknowledged. Stomach-wrenching fear threatened to leak into her voice, so she bit the inside of her cheek. Dread shot out little tentacles of hopelessness to curl around her lungs, squeezing the breath out of her. "*I'm reading you, sending help your way. What's your location?*"

"*Civic Center parking garage — A level. The building's coming apart! We need extraction.*" The voice was still urgent but the panic had faded.

She had to get her own terror under control and keep it that way, Sandy reminded herself, or she couldn't help anyone.

"*Copy you, 9-Bravo. Who am I speaking with?*"

"*Mick-*" More static, then, "*Mic-key.*"

Sandy scribbled everything she could make out into her handwritten notes. "*Mickey, you're breaking up badly. How many do you number? How long have you been trapped?*"

"*Two confirmed, dispatch, possibly three. I can feel my partner. He's not moving. I heard someone else moaning down here earlier. I don't know how long it's been. I think I've been unconscious — I'm pinned — can't move. It's dark — can't see a thing.*"

Sandy passed off the information to Ellen so her coworker could convey it to the battalion chief. The sarcastic part of Sandy's mind registered the irony of having crossed into the twenty-first century and being reduced to the mockery of a child's game of telephone.

With a pointed shake of her head, Ellen caught Sandy's eye and handed her a message from the battalion chief. As she read, Sandy's heart fluttered in her chest before moving upward to stick in her throat. Her free hand rose of its own *volition and covered her mouth, as if to prevent her from saying the words she was reading.*

The Convention Center had collapsed with several men inside. Some of them were buried under four floors of rubble, while above them the fire from the gas main explosion burned fully involved and uncontained. Rescue efforts would be delayed and prospects for extraction were grim. A chaplain was en route.

God help them all! How could she tell the man on the other end of the comm that he wasn't going to be rescued? What could she say to someone when her words were likely to be the last he'd ever hear?

* * *

Ryan kicked in the clutch and rammed the gearshift into second to take yet another turn on the series of switchbacks through the mountains. The 1967 Corvette Sting Ray had been a mess when he'd bought her, but she'd been his mess. And a bargain at the price he'd wangled. It had taken almost every one of his days off over the past two years, but he had fully restored her from the engine up. The work had been a welcome distraction from other aspects of his life.

Currently, on his first long trip in her, he was enjoying the way she held fast to the road, caressing the pavement around the twists and turns through the mountains the way a woman caressed a lover.

The throaty growl of the engine wasn't quite drowned out by the whoosh of the wind over his face. It was early in the year to drive with the top down in the mountains, but Ryan didn't care. The bracing cold reminded him he was alive.

It had been too long, the guilty whisper nagged. He should never have let his life get so far out of hand. It shouldn't have taken an emergency letter from his baby brother for him to come home and make things right with the old man.

Tires squealed just a bit when he took the downward curve a little sharply. He was in the foothills now, only a few miles to go. He'd be able to open his baby up on the two-lane once the last hill was at his back. Soon the sun would drift down into the shadowy embrace of the mountains behind him, leaving him the stars for company. Damn, he'd missed the mountains of home.

Halfway through what he recognized as the last switchback, Ryan downshifted again and punched the gas. His mind registered the apparition blocking the road in front of him a bare second before reaction set in. He stood on the brake, sending the car into a slow sideways skid and stalling the engine.

"Holy hell!"

Darts of adrenaline screamed through his veins, sending his heart into a staccato rhythm as he stared at the horse and rider in the road.

Washed in the golden blush from the setting sun, the horse reared, angrily striking out at the air between them with menacing hooves, nearly unseating his rider. With a toss of his head, the startled horse reared again, baring his teeth and screaming defiance.

The red roan colt had excellent lines, but he was clearly too much for his rider. Though the horse responded to her steady touch, it was obvious any sense of control she had was an illusion. Ryan shoved the car door open and jumped to his feet, ready to pick up the pieces when the rider was thrown. But when she swung her gaze in his direction, fury blazed in eyes the color of chicory blossoms. Her face mirrored the horse's defiance.

Sparks of awareness replaced astonishment, and a grin pulled Ryan's lips upward as he lifted a hand in greeting.

"Jackass!" The rider shoved at the wild mass of dark hair falling across her face. The motion distracted her, giving her mount the opening to misbehave.

With a clatter of edgy hooves on asphalt, the big colt danced and circled, threatened to rear again, but she recovered quickly and held him down. Then she tugged on the reins, steering the agitated horse away from the road, and sidestepping him down the steep, gravel-covered incline. Upon reaching solid footing, the colt wheeled sharply around. The rider cast a scathing look over her shoulder as the horse erupted into a reckless gallop across the prairie.

Pain shot through Ryan's neck, and he realized he'd been clenching his jaw. Absently, he rubbed the back of one hand along his chin, but he kept his eyes on the horse and rider until they were no more than a speck in the distance.

"Well," he said to the early evening sky. "I've just been schooled."

He wasn't sure if he was going to shake things up with his return or get himself shaken up. But he sure as hell planned to find out who lived behind those haunting chicory blue eyes.

Shaking his head, he started to lower himself into the car when he froze. Why was it sitting at such an odd angle? He strode around to the passenger side and groaned at the sight of the front tire, rolled right off the rim from his sideways skid.

* * *

By the time she had encountered the stranger in the fast car, Sandy's earlier upbeat mood had degraded, thanks to the dull heartache she'd given herself from lancing her old wound. Ordinarily she would have laughed off the incident and introduced herself once she'd realized no one was hurt. But the moron had just sat in his car staring in disapproval, apparently waiting for her to move out of his all-important way.

Wherever the aggravating stranger was going, she sincerely hoped he didn't so much as make a pit stop in Orson's Folly. She was pretty sure another meeting of that sort would result in her doing more than yelling at him. Pictures of strangling the shit-eating grin off his face popped into her mind.

Her heart raced with the need to dispel her jitters, and Sandy let the colt have his head again. Domingo calmed them both by doing what he loved most, streaking at breakneck pace over the plains of western Wyoming.

By the time they slowed to a walk alongside the fence leading to the stable yard, her ire at the stranger on the road had mellowed to a mildly bad memory. Whoever he was, it was likely he'd already hit Orson's Folly and driven on through. The sun rested in the cradle between the peaks of two mountains, sending lingering shafts of red to cast long shadows against the blue and white buildings. Sandy closed her eyes, bracing against the little pinprick of pain, and allowed herself to remember the reason she'd first come to Wyoming.

* * *

"You hang on, do you hear me?" she ordered. "I won't go anywhere until they have you, I swear. But you have to stay with me. Promise!"

"Okay... promise." His words were slurred, his voice weary.

Sandy struggled to think of something to talk about — to keep him speaking and alert. "Do I hear an accent, Mick?"

His laugh was slow and soft. "Yep, I'm afraid so. I can't seem to get the Wyoming out of my voice."

That worked! "Tell me about Wyoming."

He sighed. "There's nothing like a wild gallop across the plains on a fast horse. If you can be up on that horse at daybreak, you feel like you're flying up to meet the day. And to be in the Red Desert at sundown's even better. If you time it right, just a split second before the sun's gone, you feel like you're inside all that red and orange glow. Then in your next breath you're standing in pitch black. When you look up, the stars are already popping out. So many stars they blend together. And there's always shooting stars for making wishes." He laughed softly. "I guess I sound a little pathetic."

"No." She wished she could touch him with more than her voice. "More like a homesick cowboy."

He was quiet for a time, then, "I guess maybe I am, Angel. I am homesick."

His quiet admission brought tears to Sandy's eyes, and she prayed he'd see those sunrises and sunsets and stars again. "So you lived in the desert plains?"

"I had the best of both worlds," he answered, his words filled with pride. "Our ranch is in the middle of a finger of desert that's nestled between two legs of mountains and forest."

"Why did you leave?"

"That's a story for another time," he said. *"I'll tell you when we're on our first date."*

"Are you asking me out?"

"Oh, we'll go out." His voice gave her visions of an easy cowboy grin. *"I was just making the plans."*

Her lips twitched at his audacity.

* * *

Cooled and brushed, Domingo nickered a soft goodbye as Sandy left the comfort of the stable and walked into the cold night air.

Stars twinkled into view overhead, millions of glistening pinpoint lights fusing into a lacy curtain of soft illumination against the darkness. A trail of shimmery light tracked across the sky.

For the first time in seven years, her automatic wish wasn't for something impossible. "I want to feel alive again."

Emotionally and physically exhausted, she tore her eyes from the stars with a heavy sigh and climbed into the rusty Chevy pickup. It was older than she was by several years, so she counted her blessings it still ran. Driving past the main homestead, Sandy tossed a wave to Justin McGee, sitting on the wide front porch of the ranch house puffing on his nightly cigar. With a smile and a nod, the old rancher politely touched a forefinger to the brim of his battered tan Stetson.

Just as Sandy reached the cedar fenceposts marking the entrance to the ranch, a pair of headlights swung in from the main road. So, the McGee men were about to receive a caller. Maybe Sean had finally convinced Melanie Mitchell to drop by after her shift at the bar.

The two sets of headlights collided, the bright beams briefly joining forces and splitting the darkness. Then the moment was gone, leaving Sandy with a vague impression of something low and fast before she was engulfed by the cloud of dust chasing behind.

Nope. She coughed against the sting in her throat. Definitely not Mel, who tended to drive her ancient economy car with the caution of a grandmother. Tough break for Sean.

* * *

Ryan braked in front of the old ranch house and killed the engine. He popped open the door but took some deep breaths before climbing out of the car.

Though the land slumbered beneath a blanket of darkness, the nighttime couldn't mask his memories. He knew just beyond the edge of the light lay open spaces, fields of green and gold dotted by brown-and-white cattle and rolls of cut hay, all in the protective embrace of the Rocky Mountains to the west.

Closing his eyes, Ryan inhaled deeply, intoxicating himself on the aromatic blend of cow manure, freshly mown hay, and mountain wildflowers that hung in the air. The sweet, somewhat earthy scent of home.

Overhead, a shooting star blazed a fiery arc through the myriad visible stars. Ryan thought of a time, so long ago, when he and Sean had lain next to their mother on a sleeping bag, watching the stars overhead. Every time she saw a shooting star, she had urged them to make a wish.

The memory faded as suddenly as it had come. What the heck was he doing, coming back to Wyoming?

"Not much call for such a fancy machine on a ranch," admonished a gravelly voice from the porch's shadows. "But you always did love speed, didn't you, boy?"

Ryan stiffened as Justin took a step forward into the light cast by the moon.

"Hello, Dad." Ryan kept his response respectful and reserved. Leave it to his father to act like this was just another homecoming after a night in town. "You look good."

Justin chuckled. "Still spreading it thick, I see." But fondness had crept into his voice. "What I look is old." He nodded in the direction of the huge barns that had been standing since before Ryan was born. "Your brother's out there locking up... if you want to go find him, let him know you're here."

The statement startled Ryan. "Since when do McGee barns need locking?"

The old man leaned against the porch railing and examined the tip of his cigar.

Ryan waited. It was maddening, but no amount of pushing would get his father to talk before he was ready.

Finally Justin shrugged, fixed Ryan with a pointed stare. "A boy goes away for sixteen years, he's bound to see some changes when he comes back a man."

Same old shit with you, isn't, Dad? But Ryan held his tongue and acknowledged the well-deserved punch straight to the heart with a nod and a wry smile. Then he turned and strode toward the barns.

Strong floodlights, mounted at the corners of each building, lit the yard. Sean was clearly visible as he slid the barn door closed and set the lock. He walked toward the stable, a black-and-white dog at his heels.

Ryan stood just outside the light's edge watching his brother, looking for a trace of the kid he'd left behind.

The skinny boy's frame had become lean and muscular. Glow-in-the-dark blond hair had toned down some, but Ryan noticed it still had a tendency to curl at the ends even though his brother kept it cut short. Sean had been thirteen when Ryan had left. He'd grown into a man.

When Sean emerged from the stable, he ordered the dog to stay inside. Then with a flexing of his muscles, he slid the door closed. Ryan raised an eyebrow. His little brother had developed some broad shoulders and strong arms. While setting the latch, Sean's hands stilled. He eased around, his body tense, ready for anything. It had always been uncanny, the way the kid had been so acutely aware of his surroundings; it still was.

Ryan stepped into the light. Green eyes identical to his own met and held his gaze. Ryan marshaled his expression and waited, unmoving.

Sean's tension visibly drained. His smile started slowly, in his eyes first, then spreading to his mouth, where it bloomed into a full grin.

"Ry!" In two long-legged strides, Sean was in front of him. "Oh, man, it's good to see you!"

In a move too sudden for Ryan to dodge, Sean folded him into a bear hug and lifted him off his feet, his carefree laughter driving out the last vestiges of Ryan's uncertainty.

Welcome home, Ryan McGee.

Also from Dingbat Publishing

Chapter 1

Tuesday, December 7, 1813

 Fidelity Scott sucked in a shivery breath and froze, knitting needles poised like twin exclamation marks amid her neatly coiled pink yarn. All sensation faded away and around her, the morning room paled to a foggy grey nothingness. The crackling fire warmed her face but lost all color and sound, and the tremor in her hands started in her knitting needles and rippled through to her toes, missing none of her in between.

It happened every time, without fail. Her friend Clarissa Pelham had mentioned *that name*, the one guaranteed to draw Fidelity into dreamy, mindless yearnings no matter the circumstances, and it did so with its usual heady abandon. The raw emotions shivering through her seemed to suck all the bones from her body, leaving her trembling like some loathsome sea creature.

Her younger cousin, Jessica Alcock, sprawled back across the sofa, one arm falling over her face in a pretended swoon, the other grabbing for one of the overstuffed pillows propped among the cushions. The lower half of her face, all that could be seen through her amateur theatrics, seemed to melt into a gooey puddle of drool. "Oooh, yes, Mis-ter Bright-en-burg!" she trilled in a vibrato sing-song.

A chorus of sighs broke through Fidelity's name-induced fog and she shook herself awake. Embarrassing, that was. Honestly, if she couldn't control her reaction when *a certain gentleman's* name was mentioned, then she scored no higher on propriety than her two young cousins, which was very very bad indeed.

At least no one else in the morning room had managed to stay unaffected. On the chair by the hearth, Clarissa stared at the wallpaper, sewing forgotten in her lap and a dreamy expression blanking out her face. The two cousins, younger Jessica and elder Georgette, were too busy indulging each other's overly dramatic silliness to notice anyone else's. Strange, how no one was able to avoid collapsing into a pitiable, quivering mass whenever *that name* was mentioned. Of course, considering the incredible masculinity said name represented... Just the thought moved a few coals from the fireplace to somewhere deep inside her belly.

Georgette squirmed, a single indecorous wriggle of unbearable delight. Several blond curls broke free from her careless knot and dangled around her face, one sporting a forlorn hairpin that swung with her movement. "Oooh, yes, Mister Brightenburg, he of the most delicious legs. What he does to a pair of silken hose and breeches—"

Appalled, Fidelity dropped a stitch. "Georgette!" Not that it wasn't true. But saying it aloud was beyond the pale, even here in the privacy of the morning room. *Although come to think of it, it would be lovely to just hang it all and squirm along with her.*

It didn't help that her traitorous thoughts dwelled on the legs in question. Those lovely curving calves, the whipcord muscular thighs, and above that...

"Indeed!" Jessica flipped upright on the sofa and whirled, grabbing Georgette's shoulders. "Such men should be required by law to wear nothing else."

Fidelity's hands jerked and another loop slid off the needle. *Those girls can't get any worse. It's impossible.*

"Or nothing at all!"

So much for that notion.

The girls collapsed into a single pile of giggling foolishness, blond and brown hair intermixed. Heat climbed Fidelity's cheeks. She was no prude, but those two were becoming more — well, more overtly mature by the day. Thankfully Clarissa was discreet; she'd never gossip about their behavior, at least not with anyone besides Fidelity. *Which is another reason to let go and join them.*

The sudden thought startled her. *Um, no. Actually, it's not.* And now she was arguing with herself.

Fidelity cleared her throat. "Young ladies, neither of you is old enough to be noticing any such thing."

Sudden movement from Clarissa's chair, then a stillness, just as sudden.

Two pairs of blue eyes peered from the heap, artless as kittens and just as innocent. The blond head rose and Georgette propped herself on her elbows atop her sister. "And when shall we be?" she asked, ignoring Jessica's writhing beneath her. "When we're your age, cousin dear?"

Little minx. Fidelity folded her knitting and put it aside. Too much to ask, getting something productive accomplished with those two in the room. "That's unfair. There's only a handful of years between us." And yet, since their governess had left (with a discreet mop of her brow) and their mother refused to come to town, Fidelity now bore responsibility for their education and manners, ensuring their gowns and entertainments were appropriate, and chaperoning them around Mayfair. Just the thought infuriated her.

I am not some pitiful spinster. Not yet, at least.

She hid the shiver. There was nothing wrong with being unmarried at three-and-twenty. It didn't mean she'd never be loved nor have a home of her own. It only meant — well, it only meant she'd not yet married, and nothing more. The right man had come along, but—

Don't be a ninny. It means Sylvestre Brightenburg hasn't proposed yet, and that's because he hasn't noticed you exist.

Clarissa shook out her sewing, a controlled billow of white lawn. "Funny how we never forget our decorum when Mister Greysteil's name is spoken. And yet he's as handsome as Mister Brightenburg, if not more so. I challenge any young lady—" she eyed the girls meaningfully "—to dispute that."

On the sofa, Georgette froze, staring down at her still-flattened sister. Likewise, Jessica stilled her wriggling, staring back. Both creamy foreheads began puckering.

Fidelity flashed Clarissa a tiny smile. Could taming her cousins be so simple?

Then Georgette shrugged and grabbed Jessica's pillow, yanking it away. The shrieking began immediately, the renewed wriggling a second after.

"I must grant you the point, Clarissa," Georgette said through the ruckus. With one hand, she lifted the pillow overhead, out of Jessica's reach; with the other, she propped herself on her sister's midsection, keeping her pinned. "For some reason unknown to womankind, Mister Greysteil of the luscious thick hair and scrumptious green eyes simply does not attract the same level of absorption."

Annoyance flashed through Fidelity's aggravation. John Greysteil had been friends with the two related families, the Scotts and the Alcocks, since Fidelity had turned ten. He deserved more from them than a shrug and a flippant comment. But she had to admit, Georgette had scored, as well: Greysteil reduced none of them to a spineless jellyfish, not even when he smiled.

Perhaps they merely knew him too well. As male animals went, Greysteil was magnificent as a Thoroughbred stallion. But Brightenburg carried an air of mystery and superiority, power and distinction. If Greysteil was a racehorse, Brightenburg was a mustang, unreachable on some thundering Western plain.

With a herd of lusty females galloping along behind him. Fidelity stifled her snort of laughter. She'd best not share that thought.

Jessica finally shoved Georgette aside and sat up. Her hairpins could claim no more success at keeping her locks in place than her sister's; a brown coil fell to her shoulders and tangled with her fichu, which had been tugged halfway from her gown's neckline. "I challenge any young lady not to notice Mis-ter Brightenburg."

"Especially his legs," Georgette said.

More giggles. More tugging of the pillow, back and forth between them.

"You rip that pillow, and you replace it." Fidelity sighed and grabbed her knitting. She had two stitches to reinstate.

Jessica released the pillow immediately; she hated sewing. "Fi, you must admit you've noticed Mis-ter Brightenburg's physical attributes yourself."

Fidelity stiffened, a flush of heat starting in her face. "Whatever do you mean?"

The sound Georgette made could only be described as a whoop. The heat in Fidelity's face intensified.

"Young lady, that racket better becomes some wild creature—" *definitely not a horse* "—rather than a civilized gentlewoman." Granted, they were discussing Georgette. Perhaps she wasn't as cunning as Jessica; she was certainly as spirited. "And I'm sure I don't know what you mean."

Surely no one had noticed her undying devotion to Sylvestre Brightenburg. She'd been discretion itself and couldn't have given herself away.

But Jessica rolled her eyes. "Everyone knows you've set your cap for him, cousin."

The blushing heat, already profound, continued to deepen, and panic licked at her self-control. "That is an execrable expression—"

The girls froze, staring at her.

Horrified, Fidelity broke off. *That vocal sharpness — not acceptable. I'm supposed to be calm, serene, unflappable.*

Easy to appreciate and love. That temperament's my greatest asset. She sucked in a deep breath and forced her floundering emotions to heel.

Georgette hugged the pillow to her chest. Her eyes widened as if she watched some dangerous creature stalking them through the morning room. *Or as if one of those galloping mares took a wrong turn toward a cliff.*

Clarissa laid a gentle hand on Fidelity's arm. "When he enters a room, you watch him." Her voice was soft. "Never staring, never anything obvious or gauche. But the rest of us could be discussing the most scintillating subject in England and your responses vary from yes to no, with little variation in between."

She sounds like she's persuading that mare off the precipice. Nice try, Clarissa. "Are you saying everyone — everyone — has observed this?" If that were true, calming her would take more than gentle words softly spoken. Fidelity could foresee crashing through a few windows and racing down Piccadilly in a wild panic. Surely her secret was safe—

But Clarissa's small sigh blew that thought out of her head. "Next time he enters a room, Fidelity, dear, try watching the rest of the company instead."

* * * *

four days later,
Saturday, December 11, 1813

At her next opportunity, Fidelity followed Clarissa's advice. She left the entertainment five minutes later, mortified to her bones.

* * *

Thanks for reading! Dingbat Publishing strives to bring you quality entertainment that doesn't take itself too seriously. I mean honestly, with a name like that, our books have to be good or we're going to be laughed at. Or maybe both.

If you enjoyed this book, the best thing you can do is buy a million more copies and give them to all your friends... erm, leave a review on the readers' website of your preference. All authors love feedback and we take reviews from readers like you seriously.

Oh, and c'mon over to our website:
www.DingbatPublishing.Weebly.com

Who knows what other books you'll find there?

Cheers,

Gunnar Grey,
publisher, author, and Chief Dingbat

δ
Dingbat Publishing

www.ingramcontent.com/pod-product-compliance
Lightning Source LLC
Chambersburg PA
CBHW070330130626
46556CB00007B/2793